FROM THE AUTHOR OF GOLDEN SANDS

TUNDE LEYE

GUARDIANS OF THE SEAL

TLsplaceMedia

First Published in Nigeria. 2016

Published by:
TLs Place Media
Lagos, Nigeria

Illustrations by:
Ekene Ngige
Yvonne Alozie

Design by:
Lucid Creative,
www.lucidcreative.com.ng

*To the thrice Holy One, always the
source of inspiration.*

*And to David, Tinu's sweetheart.
We will see you again, when we come
to the other side.*

Acknowledgment

Guardians of the Seals took five years to write. And whilst writing is one of the most solitary vocations, writing this book has been made possible because of the people around me. First, Uche Agbai, the sensei. A conversation between friends provided the spark that became this book. My sister, Moji Adeola who was amongst the first to read my initial drafts and convinced me I wasn't biting more than I could chew with a story the scale of this book.

My editors, Kemi Ogunniyi and Lola Nwanze. In spite of the thorough job you did, and making me fight to retain every word, you made editing this work fun.

The Write Right Alumni – Dimeji Ojo, Tomi Adesina, Walter Uche, Niyi Afolabi, Harold Benson and Femi Famutimi. I call them my own Inklings.

One of the best writing couples I know, Ayo Sogunro and Folasade Lawal who offered valuable insights to this work. Abigail Anaba, it was your feedback on the draft that helped move the story from good to great. I'm eternally in your debt.

My illustrators, Ekene Ngige and Yvonne Alozie – you will not be brought before Baba Risi. Ayomidotun Freeborn of Lucid Creative for the fine cover and layout. You guys are responsible for making my writing visually appealing. I thank you.

It would have taken much longer to get to this point without the success my readers helped make my blog. To you, I am eternally grateful.

Finally, to my wife, Foluso. Thank you for believing.

IN THE BEGINNING

Luke 10:18

18. He replied, "I saw Satan fall like lightning from heaven.

Isaiah 14:12-15

12. How you have fallen from heaven,
O morning star, son of the dawn!
You have been cast down to the earth,
you who once laid low the nations!
13. You said in your heart,
"I will ascend to heaven;
I will raise my throne
above the stars of God;
I will sit enthroned on the mount of
assembly,
on the utmost heights of the sacred
mountain.
14. I will ascend above the tops of the
clouds;
I will make myself like the Most
High."
15. But you are brought down to the grave,
to the depths of the pit.

ucifer sat on his throne in the dark realm of Neatherworld as he reviewed the reports reaching him, his leathery hand on his scaly face. Thick, dark smoke filled the air, reflecting the character of the inhabitants and the master of that world. The smoke came from burning brimstone pits scattered all over the place. Lucifer routinely had demons thrown into them on nothing more than a whim. It was truly an infernal territory. His kingdom ran on fear, and that fear was sustained by ruthlessness on the part of those who ran it. At the slightest show of weakness by any in his realm, those he ruled so ruthlessly pounced without a thought.

For some time, his main reason for torturing his minions had been for the chance to see something happen, to have the pleasure of watching someone else suffer. But that was not solving the real problem. He was bored of the life in Neatherworld. After spending eons with the same set of beings in that abysmal place, he would sacrifice anything for the chance at something new. But he did not possess the power to create anything new, so the best he could do was to mould the already created sphere of Neatherworld to suit him. No other being but God had the power to create true newness, something out of nothing. And so Lucifer had to depend on his number one foe for the opportunity to experience something new. What an annoying irony. Ah! What would he not do for the joy of being Heaven's chief musician once again! But he paused and cursed himself for even allowing that thought cross his mind. He was a creature of aspiration. That had not been enough. He had aspired to greater things. Even though he had experienced setbacks in pursuing his aspirations, he saw them as just that – setbacks, from which he would bounce back. These kinds of thoughts put him in the mood to torment some unfortunate demon. The next one to come across him would be unlucky. He let out a rueful sigh as he turned his attention to other things. Someone was finally doing something new, after all this time, and he was watching every move with keen interest.

He had been closely observing the ongoing creation of the earth. Since he had been banished to Neatherworld, his one obsession had been finding a way back into Heaven. He was still convinced that if he could get in, he would be able to win more angels to his cause. Then he would take his chances again at being the Supreme Being.

"I got the most worthless one-third of the angels in that rebellion," he mumbled to himself.

One would find it hard to believe that Lucifer was once the most beautiful and desirable thing in the world. That was a memory from a time so long ago, it defied being called time. Now, he was a real monstrosity. He surveyed what he could see of his form - scaly hands that ended in claws, webbed together at bases with a green, sticky gel. The pipes on his chest that had once produced beautiful music in Heaven were now emitting nothing but evil darkness in unadulterated form. The only remnant of his angelic form was his pair of wings. And this was only his first release, his eni. He would lose even this stub of his previous estate in his second release, his eji. Whenever he released his second form, he was so purely evil that just the sight of him caused untold devastation.

Again, he took his mind away from all that to the present. All around him, demons were buzzing with energy. Each was working on a plan to spoil the perfect world that was being created. Each plan was different, just as each demon was different. Some demons were tall and others short, some big and others small, some vile-looking and others fairly good-looking, some fast-moving and others sluggish. They, like Lucifer, were seeing new and beautiful things coming into being at the Word of the Creator, the kind they had not seen since being consigned to the Neatherworld. But none of these demons knew what Lucifer was really looking out for. All the things created so far had not interested him. None of the beings created so far was the one who would have dominion over the earth. He had put his highest ranking demons on a special assignment, to monitor any unusual action by God while creating any being. Lucifer could not afford to miss any special moment.

It was the morning of the sixth day of creation and the demons had reported nothing. Lucifer was beginning to wonder if indeed this would turn out as he had predicted, that maybe God had after all become wary of entrusting any created being with such responsibility after Lucifer's rebellion.

Lucifer raised his head and saw that Guilliam, his first lieutenant, was requesting to approach his throne. Even though he knew none of these demons were powerful enough to take him on, the fact that he had tried to take God on at some point was a constant reminder to him of what ambition could drive any being to do. Needless to say, any of these demons would jump at the slightest of opportunities to overthrow Lucifer. Armed with this knowledge, Lucifer had placed the demons under strict instructions not to approach him except he beckoned on them expressly to do so. Breaching this rule brought immediate and eternal consequences for the demon that did. Few had made the mistake of breaking the rule, and those occurrences had been in the early days of the fall. Now, no one dared make the mistake. With a movement of his clawed hands, he signalled for the demon to approach his throne.

Guilliam was one of the few demons that also had an eji form. He had been a sword-bearing seraph in the old days in Heaven, one of the angels that worshipped around God's throne. He still retained many of his seraph features, but rather than the pure, shining white he would have been in Heaven, he was now a chilling black. His formerly-golden crown had become black, and so had his sword. Even his eyes were black. His six wings rested stiffly on his back and his sword dangled in a hilt at his hip. His voice sounded like a thousand voices merged and then all compressed into one person's speech. He seemed more excited than usual, and that roused Lucifer's interest, though Lucifer did not bother to show it. Guilliam approached the throne and stopped on the lowest of the twelve huge steps that led to the throne itself.

He bowed stiffly and said, "Our great Lord Lucifer, during my watch of the observation of the creation process, I took note of something that you would find extremely interesting, and I have come to speedily report it to you."

Lucifer growled. "Since you have pre-empted my interest in the report you are yet to give, what might that be?" He rested his hand on his scaly thigh and dug his claws into his skin as he waited for Guilliam to go straight to the point. These formerly high-ranking ones, he thought with displeasure, still had an illusion of the heavenly court and retained the annoying habit of speaking in circles. Their flowery language, however, was employed only when they spoke to demons stronger than them, and Lucifer was aware of that. They were extremely ruthless when in the company of low-ranking demons, and did not hesitate to subject them to all kinds of torture for any perceived disrespect. Guilliam was particularly obsessed with order and respect.

"He spoke the word and it failed!" Guilliam said excitedly, his voice filling the whole space. "The word failed!"

Lucifer could not believe his ears. That was the best news he could have ever hoped for. But he knew it was too good to be true. Hope was something a fallen angel like him could not afford to nurse, at least not in matters like this.

"The word never fails," Lucifer said casually. "The word is the sure thing that makes Him God. It is the most potent and powerful weapon in His arsenal and the true fabric by which He calls things into existence, out of nothing. Once He speaks a thing, then that thing is. Do not play on my intelligence, you fiend, by telling me things that are not possible."
Guilliam sensed trouble. "If I may explain, Lord Lucifer…"

"Oh get on with it, will you!" Lucifer roared and slammed his hands on the arm of his throne. The lower demons around scampered for cover at his wrath.

Guilliam quickly started his explanation. Encounters with his master were always unpredictable - they could end up in a promotion or a vicious punishment. "Well," he began, "so far, from our observation of the creation process, when He wanted to make anything, He would just speak the word, calling the thing out of the new earth and the thing would manifest immediately." Noticing his master's edginess, he quickly continued: "This rule applied to both the living things and the non-living things there. So in all those instances, His word worked."

Lucifer's impatience grew. He had already made his mind up to destroy some being. Now this fool made his choice easier. He got up from his throne and began to reduce the distance between himself and Guilliam.

Guilliam knew this meant trouble. He quickly got to the point to salvage what he could of the situation. "Today, while observing the creation, He called forth a creature He called man but nothing manifested. This was after He had deliberated on this creature far more than any other one He had created so far. He said He was making this creature in his own image and likeness, and that the creature would have dominion over everything on earth. It seems His word could not produce such a special and powerful creature… nothing came out of the earth."

That stopped Lucifer in his tracks. This was indeed interesting. But not interesting in the way this buffoon before him was seeing it. He knew there was something more to this man than any other creature. There was no doubt that the word worked, but there was definitely something unusual going on, something more than met the eye. That man was the creature he had been looking out for. He needed to directly monitor this one. But moving on to more immediate matters, this demon needed to be dealt with.

Lucifer turned on Guilliam, his eyes turning to the colour of the brimstone pits.

"You fool, so your confirmation of the working of the word is in the manifestations on that earth? A six-day-old earth? You are confirming the word only by what you see there? Unequivocal fool! You didn't even bother to look at the spiritual traces of the event, did you? And I call you my lieutenant? Worthless piece of trash!"

He swung his hand and there was a great crackling noise from behind Guilliam. The condemned lieutenant struggled to get away but he was rooted to the spot by a power greater than his. All the demons cleared from the area and watched from afar. They began cheering. The downfall of a lieutenant meant an opening for a lesser demon to become a lieutenant. Amongst the demons, there was no camaraderie. They were bound together only by mutual distrust and fear of one another and of their superiors, and did not hesitate to cause or applaud the destruction of another if there was gain from it.

Where Guilliam stood, the gates to any demon's worst fear opened. Neatherworld gave way and the portal to Tartarus appeared. There, he would continue falling endlessly in a world of blackness, unable to stop the fall and powerless to do anything else but fall. There would be nothing to hold on to. He would fall until he had no sense of anything. And yet, the falling would continue. He would keep falling until he lost a sense of existence. It was the worst punishment for a demon, one which lasted for eternity. Once you were in, you could never get out.

As Guilliam struggled against being sucked in, he briefly transformed into his eji form, a huge metallic replica of his eni form but with a giant seraph sword. He planted the sword into the ground and held on tightly with huge and powerful arms, trying to anchor himself in Neatherworld. But his efforts were in vain. Sword and all, he was sucked into Tartarus and the gates disappeared in an instant, like it had never been there. An eerie calm swept across the place.

Lucifer returned to his throne. "Get back to work now!" he barked. All the onlookers scampered away.

Now, he pondered, why did the word not create a manifestation for this creature? Had he been there himself, he might have been able to do a probe of the situation immediately. Things were getting interesting and it was time to leave his throne. He made preparations to get a first-hand, closer look at the earth that was being created.

The day wore on, and the afternoon turned into evening, yet nothing happened. The creatures already created on the earth were going about life as ordered by their creator. The new earth smelt of freshness and was bursting with life. There was life in the waters, in the air and on the ground. But in all this, the activity he was looking out for the most had not yet occurred. However, Lucifer knew it would be futile to stop looking now. This was a critical time, a critical creature. He would watch for as long as it took.

Then, in the cool of the evening, as the young sun was turning red in the horizon, God left His throne in Heaven to come down to earth. This was the first time in the whole creation process that this had happened. Lucifer quickly transformed into his pre-rebellion form so he could get close enough to observe. His present demon form would have been repelled by the nature of God and unable to withstand His presence.

Then Lucifer saw it. He saw God forming something out of the red clay of the earth. The Big Guy was actually soiling His hands for something. This was new. Lucifer watched on keenly. Then he saw the thing God was crafting take form. The form he observed was not anything majestic. In fact, some of the creatures that had been created by the word looked bigger and stronger. This new creature had no wings, no sword, no claws, no fangs, no weapons. Yet this creature was meant to have dominion over the vast earth. By what means? Lucifer was being distracted by his own thoughts. He again looked at the man being fashioned.

It had the form of an angel but was infinitely smaller. The smallest of Lucifer's demons could handle something of this size without even trying. So this was all that the creature, man, was - something formed out of clay and so small, so small he could smash it with just his breath. But he kept on looking. Something kept him from looking away. He couldn't explain what it was but he could feel it. Something was really about to happen, something that had never happened before, something that God had never done before.

God moved close to the creature, so close His mouth was over the creature's nostrils. And then He breathed into the creature. As He did, the man became a living soul, possessing an essence of God. Only God could have crafted such a plan. Even Lucifer was impressed. Something so simple was the greatest of all creation, even greater than the most powerful of the angels. No demon, not even he, could handle this creature head on. The very essence of God was within the creature. Nothing was created greater. So this was what God desired. He wanted relationship. He wanted something that could relate with Him out of its own will, out of love.

Lucifer watched as God carried the man tenderly in his arms and placed him inside a garden He had planted in preparation for him. He called the garden Eden of the East. It was replete with all kinds of lush trees in full fruit, all looking juicy and ready for the man to dig into. A river ran right through it, dividing into smaller rivers just at the edge of the garden. The jealousy in Lucifer rose. He couldn't create anything like this. He watched on in awe. Then he heard God speak to the man.

"You are free to eat from any tree in the garden," He said, "but you must not eat from the tree of the knowledge of good and evil, for when you eat of it, you will surely die."

Lucifer had seen enough. Unlike him and any other creature, this one called man was free to do things according to his own will. This creature had freewill. Lucifer felt the rage within him begin to grow. He needed to get out of there before he lost his form. He quickly crossed the spirit divide and that took him back to his realm in Neatherworld. As he entered, he released his eji form. He destroyed everything that was in his path. Countless demons that could not get out of his way quickly enough were consumed by the smoke spewing out of his chest pipes. All that fell within his shadow as he passed was obliterated the instant the shadow touched them. Why did God have to have it all? He had Heaven and now He had created a very beautiful earth, plus man, with whom He could have a relationship. And what did he, Lucifer, have? This smoke-filled, depressing place, and demons that were the vilest of all things in the universe, as companions.

Well then, he needed to figure out how to use what he had to get what he wanted. He needed a demon that would be small enough to be attached to Eden of the East. He called Nimrod, a wiry, tiny demon, to himself. Nimrod looked as if his head was entirely made up of an eye and two huge, floppy ears. A small horn rose out of the centre of his forehead, right above his single eye.

"Go and keep a watch on that garden," Lucifer instructed. "And report everything that happens there to me. Leave nothing out! Absolutely nothing! Now go!"

The first report that came to Lucifer was that the newly-created man had been asked to name every creature on earth. Hmmm. The Old Spirit. Lucifer knew that you established dominion over a thing by naming it. So God was really giving this man dominion, he pondered. He had to do something about it.

The next report was even more alarming. Nimrod was a low-ranking demon, so he went straight to the point without the finery the more senior demons employed. "God has made a help-meet for the man," he said. "She's like him in every way, except she's more delicate. He calls her woman and has a soft spot for her. It seems he would do anything for her."

"And how is their relationship with the Old Guy going?"

"He now comes down to the man and woman in the garden every day in the cool of the evening, just to spend time with them. However, the portal He comes down through is known only to the man and woman and the keys to the portal are with Him. We cannot infiltrate heaven through that route."

"And who gave you the guts to tell me what we can or cannot do?" Lucifer barked as he leaned forward on his throne. The little demon cowered and shook in unbridled fear, expecting the worst.

"Get out of here and back to work!" Lucifer ordered.

Nimrod jumped at the chance to escape this encounter unscathed. He slunk away from his master and disappeared into the surrounding darkness in an instant. Lucifer processed what he had heard. God had opened a portal into heaven. If a certain someone could come down through it, then a different someone could also go into heaven through it. He needed to observe this new companion for himself – the woman. He began to formulate a plan. It was high time he visited Eden of the East again.

Eden was beautiful. The sun shone clearly in the sky like a beacon of warmth, shedding life-giving sunlight to all the creatures of the garden. The man, who had called himself Adam, and the woman, now called Eve, both spent the mornings tending the garden. And then they waited in the evening for God to come down. Lucifer had taken on the form of a snake to blend into the environment. Adam and Eve spent some time chatting away with the animals too, for in those early days of the earth, men and animals could understand each other's tongues. And they had wonderful conversations together. Gradually, Lucifer got closer and closer to the woman, and she spent more and more time talking with him more than any other animal in the garden.

One evening, after God had left for the day, and Adam rested by the banks of the River Pishon- one of the rivers the main river broke into, Lucifer sought Eve out. In no time, they were wandering together in the garden and chatting away. Their conversation was particularly animated, as they talked about God.

Lucifer asked, "So where does God go everyday when He leaves you and Adam?"

Eve laughed. "Heaven of course. Where else? Oh get off it, everyone knows that." She laughed again.

Lucifer let out a hissing sound. It was really a hiss of disgust, but as serpents always hissed, Eve could not tell. "Ever been to heaven before?" he asked her.

"No I haven't," she answered as she reached for a juicy pear in the tree above them. Little creatures raced through the brush all around them and a small owl sat in the tree. It was not yet dark, but the moon had become visible in the sky. It was a new moon.

Lucifer wrapped himself playfully around her, making sure she couldn't leave as he spoke. "Can I tell you a secret?" he asked.

Eve nodded her head to signify a yes as she chewed on her fruit and savoured the juice released into her mouth. This serpent could be so playful.

"I have been there before," he hissed into her ears.

"You?" she asked with surprise. "Been where? No one on earth has been there before."

"Is that what you think? Who have you asked?" Lucifer's tongue was darting in and out of his mouth in quick succession.

"Well, no one. Never saw a need to ask. I'll ask Adam. Ah, Adam. I should get going. I'll see you tomorrow. Unwrap now." She laughed.

Lucifer smiled and hissed as he watched her go. He knew he had planted the seed of wonder in her heart. It would grow slowly and steadily. In the meantime, he needed to get to Neatherworld to prepare the demons. Soon, the earth would be his and he needed them ready.

"Nimrod, let's go," Lucifer said.

A small cricket crept out of the garden undergrowth and hopped onto the back of the snake as the snake slithered to the edge of the garden. Once there, both snake and cricket transformed into their eni forms. With a sweeping movement of Lucifer's hands, the portal to Neatherworld was opened to them and they made the spirit jump across the two worlds.

Eve found Adam bathing in the Pishon. He was in the water up to his waist. The animals of the waters and the bank seemed to have retired for the night and Adam was alone. She took a dive and joined him. The water was soothing and the night sky was clear, with a sprinkling of stars surrounding the bright moon.

Eve snuggled up to Adam. He smiled. "How's my woman," he asked. "You sure need a bath dear; you haven't bathed since the day's work." His voice was clear and rich, a soothing baritone that caressed his woman's ears.

Eve threw her hair back, laughing. "I join my man in the water, and all he can think about is a bath." She paused to look into his eyes and cupped his face in her hands.

He shook his head. "Interesting. I thought the serpent was great company." He kissed her lightly.

"But there are things that only a man can do, you see," Eve said. She led him out of the water, moving sensually in front of him.

His eyes were fixed on her for a brief moment before he rose out of the water after her. She was indeed beautiful. God had made her so well. Adam made sweet, passionate love to her on the river bank.

Back in the fiery Neatherworld, Lucifer called the demons together. He was back in his eni form. Some of the lesser demons would be unable to survive his eji form, and he needed all the manpower he could muster for his plan. If he could get that portal open long enough for his army to rush into heaven, he can lay ambush on the faithful angels. Then, the ones that are spared would decamp to him out of fear and God would be left all alone. Lucifer allowed himself the faintest of smiles, animating his grotesque face briefly. As the demon assembly gathered, a swirling, milling sea of dark forms all around him, he mounted his throne, his eyes like fire. He curled his fist into a ball and slammed it into the arm of his throne and his whole body glowed.

"It must work!" he snarled.

The demons maintained a clear distance from him. Even in this assembly, none came so close to him as to be able to make any contact with him. Gatherings like this festered rebellion and Lucifer had taken necessary precautions. One could never be too careful when it came to his kind of underlings.

He rose to address the assembly. "Comrades in the struggle, the time for the actualisation of our dreams is near. I shall tell you something that only a few beings know and that has been hidden from the beginning of the ages. I have chosen to call you together and articulate it to you like this, rather than disseminate the information through spirit communication. This is because of the importance of what I am about to say. It is a secret so powerful, that even the few that know it dare not speak of it, for the fear of the consequences from the One that the secret is about. But I have decided to let you in on this secret, as my comrades. Most of you know God as the all-powerful being whose word is omnipotent, whose vision is omnipresent and whose mind is omniscient. But it was not always so. No, it wasn't! God was once an angel, like every single one of us once was!"

A murmur went through the crowd. He paused and surveyed his audience. They were listening with rapt attention now, from the lowest to the highest.

"Before the making of the assembly of angels, there were only the Elder Angels existing, each of us equal in statue and in power," Lucifer continued. "There were only ten of us. You all know Michael, Gabriel and Raphael. They were also Elder Angels. God was one of the ten Elder Angels. His name was Yahweh. But in those pre-time periods, His quest for discovery led Him to search for ways to make Himself greater. He discovered the Tree of Almightiness and ate of its fruit. Eating of the fruit transformed Him from a mere angel into the Almighty God that you all know. But I knew Him before He became God and know He was not always all powerful. So while I served Him, I also sought to find the Tree of Almightiness. After searching for ages and ages, during which you all came into being, I found it. But just as I was on the verge of tasting the fruit of my labour, God came and accused me of wanting to be like Him. Of course I wanted to be like Him! Didn't He want anyone to be like Him? Even as I speak to you now, doesn't the desire to be like Him grow within you now that you know the possibility exists? What is the sin in that?"

Resounding shouts of No! No! No! rent the air. He raised his hand for quiet.

When they had all calmed down, he went on. "At that point, you, my comrades, joined me, and for that singular reason, He banished us all from Heaven. But I, your great leader was not defeated. I lost that battle, but not the war. Now, a new battle, a decisive battle, is around the corner. God has slipped up by putting his greatest treasure in those fragile earthen vessels He called men, and by so doing He has placed in our hands a golden opportunity to take back what is rightfully ours. We shall create a heaven where there is no one that is God, and every demon is equal as it was in the days of the Elder Angels. Be prepared! Be! Very! Prepared!"

Every demon let out a deafening roar, the sound of which, together, was as the most horrible sound imaginable. When they were dismissed, Nimrod made his way back to the garden. Things were indeed about to be taken up a notch.

Eve lay snuggled up to Adam's side with her arms across his chest. She enjoyed these times together with him. "Ever been to Heaven?" she asked him.

"No. Why do you ask?" Adam took in the fresh smell of her hair mixed with the scent of the earth and the river on whose banks they lay.

"Just wondering what the place where God lives is like. It's so wonderful when we are in His presence. Wonder how it would be at His place."

"Hmmm," murmured Adam. "Why don't we ask if He could take us there tomorrow evening?"

"I would like that very much. I'm so excited."

Then Adam covered her lips with a kiss and there were no more words heard at the river bank for some time.

Nimrod sent a swift report back to Lucifer without leaving Eden, by spirit communication. "They intend to ask God to take them to heaven tomorrow my Lord. What should I do?"

"I will come there to monitor things myself then," Lucifer replied. "You will mess this up on your own with your low intelligence and it's an opportunity too precious to waste."

The next evening, after God had left, Lucifer found Eve close to the centre of the garden, under an apple tree. He sank his fangs into an apple and offered it to her. "Hello madam, how are you doing today?"

"Very well, thank you," Eve replied. "And you?"

"What can a serpent do except be very well? Anyway, the buzz in the garden was that you were going to Heaven today. What happened? Were you refused entry?"

"Yes. God asked us to hold on; he said the time for our trip to Heaven was not now. We will go to Heaven in due time."

Lucifer moved forward, encouraging her to follow him. "Just as I expected," he said. "He won't let you into heaven. Anyway, I know another way in, since I've been there before. But I guess you can wait for his time as He instructed."

Eve pulled his tail. "I'll just wait. It can't be that long."

"You're naïve. It's because you will become fully like Him when you get to heaven… that's why He doesn't want you to go to heaven. I'm sure He also told you not to eat from this tree."

Eve looked up. They were in front of the Tree of the Knowledge of Good and Evil. It was a silver-coloured tree with plump, round, white fruits hanging on it. The earth around it was well tended and cleared of any undergrowth. Beside it was a twin tree, a white tree with silver-coloured fruits, almost identical to the Tree of the Knowledge of Good and Evil. It was the Tree of Life. Eve quickly stepped back. They were not to eat of the fruit of the tree.

Lucifer smirked. "See what I am saying. He told you that because you will become like Him when you eat it. Your eyes will become open, knowing good and evil by yourself. You won't need anyone to tell you right from wrong."

He went up the tree and came back down with a fruit. The fruit looked so good, so appealing. He gave it to her. "That's your key to being like the God you love so much, and going to heaven."

She hesitated briefly before she took the fruit and ate it. It tasted as good as it looked. She closed her eyes and enjoyed the taste for a few seconds. By the time she opened her eyes, it was as if her old eyes had been replaced with new ones. Everything looked different; things seemed to have taken on a harsher note. She looked around and saw the serpent holding up the fruit to her. "I feel different," she said dryly.

"That's the God perspective beginning to creep up on you," Lucifer responded.

"Everything looks different," she stated again as she tried to come to terms with that reality.

"You are beginning to see things the way they really are," Lucifer reiterated. "Now, don't enjoy this alone. Adam too should partake of this divine nature."

"Ah, yes, Adam my darling." Eve rushed to where Adam was. He wasn't too far away. She offered him the fruit.

"Eve what is this?" Adam asked. "You know we shouldn't eat this." But Eve repeated Lucifer's words to Adam. She did such a great job of convincing Adam that Lucifer saw he didn't need to do anymore. Adam ate the fruit too.

Nimrod was enjoying the new state of things. There in Neatherworld, Lucifer had given him command of the entire demon population. His small body quivered as he bellowed orders out. He flew over the array of demons, big and small, ready to rush into Heaven at his command. He contacted his master through spirit communication. "All is ready my lord; we will rush in at your word."

"Do not disturb me, fool," Lucifer barked back in the spirit. "Just wait for my orders." Then he turned to the couple before him. They looked so scared. They were realising that they were naked, for the first time. He enjoyed watching their struggle to cover themselves with leaves – leaves that would rot in no time. Fools. God really had made a mistake with these ones.

Lucifer went in for the kill. "The next thing now is to enter Heaven," he said to Adam. "Why don't you proceed to meet God at the portal so he can see your transformation into Godhood? He would be glad to see His creation evolving right before His eyes, you know?"

Clad in their leaves, Adam and Eve led Lucifer to the portal. It was a stone at the point where the main River of Eden split into four. Lucifer couldn't believe that the answer to his quest had been in plain sight for so long. He glided into the undergrowth and watched. Soon, the portal would open and with it, his window of opportunity. He double-checked with Nimrod to ascertain that his forces were ready, his tongue flicking out left and right. He had to trust that God would be distracted enough with dealing with these people so that he could make his move unnoticed.

Adam wondered why he felt uneasy about that day's meeting with God, which would soon begin. He reasoned that it could not be a bad thing to want to be like God. But his heart kept telling him he had made the worst mistake of his life. Suddenly, from out of the keystone, a familiar bright light began to shine. The light grew till it engulfed the whole of Eden, creating a warmth that was usually refreshing for Adam. Today, it felt different- the warmth was more of a heat, scorching his skin. He looked to Eve and saw that she was feeling the same way. Quickly, they tried to take cover amidst the trees in the garden. The more leaves they had around them, the more cover they hoped to get for their nakedness. But the leaves were not helping.

The presence was suffocating Lucifer. He gathered all his might and tried to connect with Nimrod spiritually. But no matter how hard he tried, he could not get any signal. For once, he regretted he ruled his realm by fear. He knew for sure that Nimrod would never take initiative. Fear of the consequences of acting out on Nimrod's own initiative would incapacitate him and cause him to wait for a command that would never come. Lucifer readied himself for the inevitable.

Genesis 3:9-24

9. But the LORD God called to the
man, "Where are you?"

10. He answered, "I heard you in the
garden, and I was afraid because I was
naked; so I hid."

11. And he said, "Who told you that you
were naked? Have you eaten from the tree
that I commanded you not to eat from?"

12. The man said, "The woman you put
here with me—she gave me some fruit from
the tree, and I ate it."

13. Then the LORD God said to the
woman, "What is this you have done?"
The woman said, "The serpent deceived
me, and I ate."

14. So the LORD God said to the
serpent, "Because you have done this,
"Cursed are you above all the livestock
and all the wild animals!
You will crawl on your belly
and you will eat dust
all the days of your life.

15. And I will put enmity

between you and the woman,
and between your offspring and hers;
he will crush your head,
and you will strike his heel."
16. To the woman he said,
"I will greatly increase your pains in
childbearing;
with pain you will give birth to
children.
Your desire will be for your husband,
and he will rule over you."
17 To Adam he said, "Because you
listened to your wife and ate from the tree
about which I commanded you, 'You must
not eat of it,'
"Cursed is the ground because of you;
through painful toil you will eat of it
all the days of your life.
18 It will produce thorns and thistles for
you,
and you will eat the plants of the field.
19. By the sweat of your brow
you will eat your food

until you return to the ground,

since from it you were taken;

for dust you are

and to dust you will return."

20 Adam named his wife Eve, because she would become the mother of all the living.

21. The LORD God made garments of skin for Adam and his wife and clothed them.

22. And the LORD God said, "The man has now become like one of us, knowing good and evil. He must not be allowed to reach out his hand and take also from the tree of life and eat, and live forever."

23. So the LORD God banished him from the Garden of Eden to work the ground from which he had been taken.

24. After he drove the man out, he placed on the east side of the Garden of Eden cherubim and a flaming sword flashing back and forth to guard the way to the tree of life.

PROLOGUE

ara held up the pregnancy test result one more time. She had imagined a thousand and one times how it would feel when her experiments finally succeeded, but nothing prepared her for the emotions that welled up within her. She had finally done it! She would go down in history as the woman who freed her gender from the shackles men had placed on them.

She had to see Lamela urgently. It was Lamela who had introduced her to The Place. She reached for her phone and dialled Lamela's number from memory.

"Hello Tara," she heard Lamela's almost masculine voice say.

"Lamela!" Tara shrieked into the receiver. "It worked. I'm pregnant! All by myself! No man involved!"

"Calm down Tara," Lamela replied curtly. "Explain to me in real sentences."

Tara rolled her eyes. Lamela was always like that- naturally hardly excitable, always cool, calm and collected. Tara tried to get a grip on herself. She was a world-famous scientist after all, and such unabashed excitement was unbecoming of her. "Autogamous reproduction in the female of the human species is now confirmed possible," she stated with better composure. "I have just successfully made myself pregnant without the use of sperm or any male cellular components. It's a girl. Men are no longer a necessary evil; we can perpetuate the human race on our own."

"You used yourself as a test subject, Tara?"

"Yes, I had a brain wave and couldn't find a test subject quickly enough."

"Why didn't you run it by me first?"

"Lamela, are we going to argue about this and lose sight of the magnitude of my discovery? Come on! I'm going to start experiments for phase two of the plan. Now that we don't need men, we can as well do away with them. Isn't that what we want?"

"Of course," Lamela replied edgily. "It is. Pardon me… I'll be with you shortly." Then she hung up.

Lamela's response worried Tara a little, but she ignored it.

When Lamela finally joined her in the lab with a group of people, Tara thought she was finally going to meet the elusive partners Lamela always referred to with whom she owned The Place. From the periphery of her vision, she observed that all her attendants were leaving the lab. She also noticed when she turned around that three of the six people that Lamela had brought in were men. That didn't make any sense.

"What are these men doing here?" she protested vehemently.

"Shut up!" Lamela replied roughly.

Before Tara could wonder what was going on, the men had surrounded her and held her down.

"You are naïve, dear Tara," Lamela said. "You have bought yourself a lease of life by using yourself as the test subject though."

The other women began to chant, a rasping, reptilian sound. Suddenly, a chilling breeze swept across the room. As the chants reached a crescendo, Lamela morphed into the most hideous creature Tara had ever seen.

"Know that I will be watching you closely, Tara," Lamela warned sinisterly. "You are precious because of the child you carry but if you give me a reason to, I will kill you myself." She paused for a moment to revel in Tara's fright. Then she ordered, "Take her away!"

And so, Tara's nightmare began.

ONE

ara always surprised herself with the way her smiles fled from her face the moment she was certain no one was watching. She was glad that she worked in a lab. That way, the only people she had to interact with regularly were her colleagues and with those, she had perfected the art of smiling on demand. None of them would have guessed the immense sadness she carried within her. That sadness. It became thicker as the day progressed and by the time she had to leave the office, it had become a dread that almost paralysed her. Everyday she told herself she would not return to the house. Every single day, she convinced herself that she would run away. And every day, her resolve failed as soon as she stepped out of the lab into the streets. She always went back to him.

"You have a date today, Tara?" She turned her head, and in that motion, her mask came back on. She was back in the lab, smiling, by the time her eyes met Lamela's. She recalled the first day she met Lamela. She had been intimidated by the woman. Lamela was everything she wanted to be. She was the authority in modern Gametology, the genius who had finally cracked the cure to cancer using gametes harvested from donors and owned the biggest lab on the continent. The lab did not recruit conventionally too. Before they contacted you, they would have thoroughly researched you and passed you through rigorous selection criteria. They only contacted you to make you an offer after they were satisfied they wanted you. No one had ever refused their offer. She felt privileged to be amongst the select few who worked for Lamela.

"Ah, the mister doesn't take housewives like me on dates any longer. That's for hot, single CEOs like you?" Tara responded with a twinkle in her eye.

"Well, like I've always told you Tara, if this mister will not take you out, then find someone else who will," Lamela said, winking.

"What, Lamela," Tara said, in mock horror. "Are you suggesting that I have an affair?"

Lamela laughed, a precisely pitched laugh, perfect like everything else about her. "Well, don't say I didn't try," she responded and then turned towards the door. She took a few steps towards the door and then paused and turned around and said "you're very beautiful, Tara. I hope he tells you so."

Tara felt the heat rise to her cheeks as she struggled for a response. She had taken off her mask too quickly as Lamela turned away and had been caught completely off guard. Before she could gather herself together, Lamela turned and was out of the lab. Slowly, she began to pick her things as she prepared to go home.

Anthony "Chubby" Cole proudly showed his brother the tattoo across his right side. It was an exact replica of the one on Alex's chest. He had paid a small fortune to get his big brother's tattoo. He wasn't prepared for Alex's reaction.

"Chubby, how did you get this? What were you thinking?" Alex was visibly angry.

"I went to a tattoo artiste, paid, winced in pain as he pricked my skin repeatedly and…"

"Quit being sarcastic mister. I'm dead serious here." Alex said sternly.

"I just thought I'd surprise you and get a tattoo exactly like yours. Why are you angry?" Tony responded, perplexed. He couldn't understand why his brother was so upset by this. They had not seen eye to eye since he joined the bikers and he was hoping to try to mend fences with this. He sincerely missed his big brother

Alex understood that Tony was always trying to be him. Since their parents died, he had been everything to his little brother – Mother, father, brother – so it wasn't surprising that Tony followed him in all things. But this wasn't something to joke with. He pressed Tony "Which tattoo artist did you go to for the tattoo? How did he know how to draw this particular tattoo flawlessly?"

Tony didn't answer. Why was this so important to his brother? "I'm asking you a question Anthony!" Alex said.

When his brother called him Anthony, then it was really serious. Tony didn't delay any further. "I only wanted to surprise you, I didn't mean to get you angry," he started.

"I'm listening," Alex interjected.

"I took a picture of your tattoo while you slept. With that, it was easy to find a tattoo artist who gave me what I wanted," Tony explained.

"Did anyone else see the picture or the tattoo when you were done?" Alex asked.

"No one else. It was a pricey and private place so only the tattoo artist saw it."

"Great. You are going to show me the place," Alex said.

"Is there something about this tattoo you are not telling me? It's just a bloody tattoo and I can get it removed if it's such a big deal." Tony said, exasperated.

There was an awkward silence between them. Alex let out a sigh. He knew this definitely looked like overreacting to his brother. But he could not explain without putting Tony in danger. Better to get him angry than that. He would apologize later.

"I do not have to explain myself to you, Anthony," he started.

"And neither do I!" Tony interjected angrily. He turned and stormed out of the room. Then, as if he thought better of it out of respect for his brother, he returned into the room, still visibly angry.

Alex continued in measured tones. "I see you have not completely lost your manners. You are not a kid anymore, Anthony. I expect you should be able to deduce quickly when something is important and yet needs to be kept discrete and not made a scene of. This, is one of those things."

Chided, Tony responded in a tone reflective of his brother's. "You've always told me everything brother. So you must understand now that I find it hard to comprehend what's so important about a tattoo, that you can't tell me plainly."

"I understand Chubby. I ask that you also understand that I am unable to tell you more. At least not now. But it is important I get to where you got the tattoo and everyone who you've shown it to."

"Okay" was all the response that Tony gave.

Lamela entered the conference room, trying her best not to notice the stares from the occupants of the room. She hated these meetings, but she could do nothing about attending so she braced herself for the grilling. There were six people seated around the fine mahogany conference table. The table had an antique telephone as its only adornment. One of the three men in the room sat at the head of the table and it was him that spoke first as soon as Lamela took her seat at the opposite end of the table "Why is the plan moving along so slowly? How long is it going to take you to drive a mere human to despair and into your arms?" His voice was gravelly and grated her ears.

"Precisely because she's human. There are rules if we are to remain in this world, and one of them is that we must not violate freewill. So, dear Iblis, until she gets driven to that point, I keep driving." It annoyed her that he had been made leader of this team by their supreme leader but she had to live with it until she got her chance. And that hinged on succeeding at this task that was now dragging.

"Perhaps you need some help to get the job done" the other lady at the table said in a patronizing tone.

"You will keep your fangs out of my subject, Batibat," Lamela snapped. Briefly, an apparition of a huge bat baring its fangs appeared behind Batibat.

"Ladies, let's not get overexcited now," Iblis said and the apparition disappeared as quickly as it had appeared. Lamela relaxed back into her chair. She hated the limits this body placed on her.

Iblis continued "your subject, as you have so scientifically put it, was merely assigned to you Lamela. And if we conclude you cannot deliver, nothing stops a reassignment. You have not forgotten how important getting her work completed is to the master's grand plan, have you?"

That patronizing tone again belying Iblis' perception of his own superiority. "I have a plan. She will be all mine and will make the decision sooner than you all think. We will then move her from the lab to The Place to focus on the work. The master's plan will be fulfilled and through her work alone," she responded. The part she left unsaid, but that was well understood at the table was that it would also mean through her own work and she would make sure the master knew this.

"You have two more weeks, Lamela. After that, you must introduce Batibat to your subject, and she will take over from there"

"No you can't!" Lamela shouted, springing to her feet.

Iblis remained calm on his seat. "I can and I will. Except you want to go and explain to the master in person. I will be glad to arrange that on your behalf", he said, smiling with his eyes closed and head cocked to the side. Lamela sat down and seethed. There was nothing she could do. "I'll make sure it's done within two weeks," she said in a more subdued voice.

"Good," Iblis responded.

"If there's nothing else, I'd like to take my leave," she said.

"Please go ahead," Iblis said politely.

She got up and went to kiss him on both cheeks before taking her leave.

"Batibat, if you ever get ahead of yourself like that again, I will make sure the master hears things. Your lack of control there nearly jeopardized the plan." Iblis said menacingly.

"Taken, dear leader. It won't happen again," Batibat responded.

"Do you think we should watch her more closely?" One of the men who had been silent all through Lamela's stay asked. He was the youngest looking of the lot.

"No Karis. She will fail and we will finish what she started. The glory for completing it will be ours and the master will reward us all." They all nodded in agreement. "This meeting is dismissed," he said, rising.

Lamela fumed in the back of her car as she whipped out her phone. She dialled a number from memory and waited for it to connect. The moment it did, she didn't bother with any greetings.

"We need to do something drastic. We are running out of time," she said curtly.

The male voice that responded was a rich baritone. "She's almost at the tipping point. We don't need her running mad or anything. If I do anything drastic now, that might just happen. I'm already giving her nightmares and all. That's already nearly crossing the line".

"You are not listening to me," Lamela growled. "You are being careful when we are running out of time. Look, the board just gave us two weeks. We either deliver her, or they pull the plug on the whole operation and someone else takes over. I don't want to face the master in those circumstances and I'm sure you don't want to either"

There was silence on the other end of the line. "Are you there?" she checked her phone. It was still connected. "Maxwell, are you there?"

"Yes," he responded "I was just shocked that Iblis would take such a drastic position."

Lamela sighed. "He's trying to screw us over. Like his boss, Nimrod, he wants us to fail and then come to finish what we've cultivated for such a long time and take glory before the master. We cannot allow this happen," she said.

"That worm. I will get him once I discard this body," Maxwell said angrily

"In due time, Maxwell. But now, we have to focus on the problem at hand. She is still hiding that she is pregnant from you. That's the lever. I want you to use it to drive her over the line." Lamela said

"Are you sure about this?" Maxwell asked. He was concerned that the situation was about to cause Lamela to act without thinking.

"Absolutely." Then she proceeded to share the plan with him in meticulous detail. There could be no mistakes.

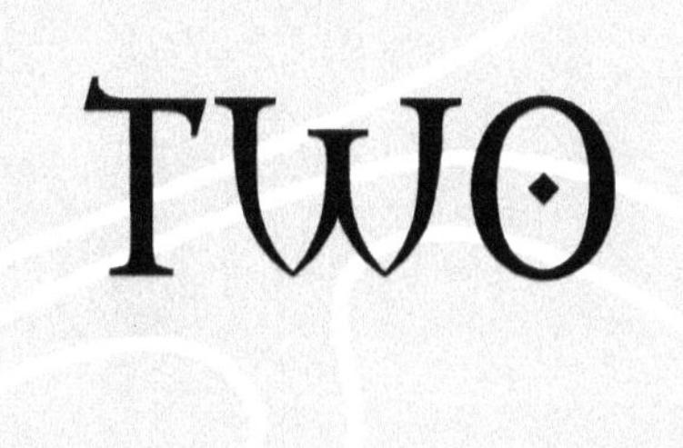

TWO

ara paused before the door, as a thousand fears ran through her mind. Every time she drove into the house, she felt like dark shadows were watching her. Sometimes, it even seemed she saw the shadows moving in the periphery of her vision and her skin began to crawl. By the time she gets to the door, the fear would have taken over her. It had not always been this way. Marrying Maxwell had initially been the escape into bliss from the horror of living with her father. She watched him beat her mother almost everyday while treating her like royalty. That is, until she turned twelve. Then he stopped treating her like his princess, and started to treat her like her mum. She had told her mum to run away with her but the woman refused. She began to despise her mum for being so weak. Then she began to make plans to run away on her own. One day, her mum discovered the plans and told her father. He had beaten her especially brutally that day. Her feelings for her mum moved from despising her to hatred. But she reserved a special hatred in her heart for her father.

The door opened and Maxwell's huge frame blocked the doorway. "Are you going to stand in front of the door forever and keep muttering to yourself like a mad woman?" He boomed as his face twisted into a menacing scowl. She took a step back to get out of his reach. She didn't realize she had been standing there for so long.

He stepped aside, making way for her to enter the house. She picked her steps gingerly, careful to make sure she didn't make any contact with him. She heard him shut the door. And then she heard him lock it. Her heart nearly jumped out of her mouth.

He could feel her fear. He liked the feeling of making her this afraid. He took his time to turn around, savouring it. Then he strode to the couch and sat in it, watching as she waited for him to say something. "Sit down" he said.

She slowly let herself into the chair opposite him, putting the table between them.

"When were you going to tell me?" he asked.
Tara felt her heart quicken. "Tell you what?" she asked weakly.

"Oh, so we answer questions with questions now eh?" he said, raising his eyebrow.

"Oh no, I didn't mean it that way," she said apologetically. Inside, she felt her disgust with herself rising. She was apologizing again for nothing. She had despised her mother for being too weak to leave her father. But here she was, in the same position, financially independent of her husband, yet she did not leave.

"That baby you are carrying is not mine. Of course you couldn't tell me you were pregnant because you knew it." Then he stood up, went around the table and stood in front of her. "Start talking" he whispered.

"It's not what you think. I didn't do anything wrong. I don't even know the father." She knew she was sounding disjointed but she kept talking. A slap silenced her.

"So you had immaculate conception? How don't you know the father? You will tell me who the bastard is. And here's what I'm going to do. I will kill you first. And then I will go and kill him. That will teach you not to cheat on me".

She flew into full panic mode. It was finally happening. He was going to kill her and her baby. Her eyes darted all over the room, searching for a way of escape. He was blocking the only way. Except she could get across the table. She decided to make a dash for it.

Without warning, she leapt out of the chair and rolled over the table. The moment she landed on her feet, she sprang forward. She had only a moment before her chance was gone. He was already swinging round the table to cut her off. She made it as far as the door. As she struggled to unlock the door, he caught up with her. She was about to scream when he hit her and everything went black.

Gabriel stood in the garden, watching everything going on in the little house. He itched to intervene, to help Tara. But he could not. Just as free will limited the other side, it limited him too. Except she called for his help from her own free will or there was an explicit overriding order from above, all he could do was watch. He looked to the west. Another storm was gathering amongst the Guardians. But this was where his orders told him to stay. He hoped the Guardians would be able to deal with what came.

Karis discarded the business suit he had worn to the meeting as soon as he got into his apartment and got into his leather and jeans riding gear. He checked his phone for the first time that evening. A message from Chubby was waiting for him. He typed a quick reply to say he'd be there shortly, dashed to his bike and rode out to join the rest of his biker posse at the warehouse he had procured for tonight.

Chubby had planned to show off his tattoo to his biker friends today. But after his brother's reaction and having to take him to the tattoo shop, he decided to keep it to himself, at least for now. He didn't really understand what his brother had gone to do at the shop. He didn't speak with anyone, not even the tattoo artist. He just looked around and sat in the area for a while. He had seemed satisfied and that was that. Tony was glad that visit had ended quickly. Karis had promised them a special time tonight and he wasn't going to miss it for anything. As he pulled up in front of the warehouse they had converted into their headquarters, the party was in full swing already. He found space for his bike in the midst of almost a hundred other bikes scattered all over the place.

"And I thought you were here already," a familiar voice called out to him above the din. He turned to see the handsome face of Karis beaming at him. Whatever anyone else said about them, this group was where he felt the most accepted. Before he met Karis and joined them, he was the chubby boy who didn't fit in. All that had since changed.

"Well, I still technically got here before you," he responded, returning the smile.

"Ready for tonight?" Karis said as he handed out a strip of colourful paper to him. They called it, the "Illuminator". Everyone got one at the door of the warehouse and was required to sniff it before going in. Not like you had to be forced to sniff it once you did it once. It gave you an unparalleled high. Sometimes you even saw dinosaurs and stuff. The thing was potent.

As they entered, everyone hailed Karis. With him by their leader's side, it always added to his high. By the time they got to the podium in front and the DJ turned down the music, Tony was seeing different creatures flying all over the warehouse. One seemed to look straight at him like it really saw him. For a moment, a chill ran through him as their eyes met. But he reminded himself it was just the high and he laughed at himself for being scared.

"Let us begin!" Karis screamed into the microphone
All of them gathered shouted "yes" in one thunderous, drug-fuelled voice.

Tara's eyes opened slowly as she regained consciousness. Her head throbbed. She tried to move but she felt restraints on her hands and feet.

"Finally, she wakes up," she heard Maxwell's familiar baritone. Suddenly the memories came rushing back.

"How long was I out for?" she asked weakly.

"Not very long. I didn't hit you too hard," he responded
When she didn't say anything he came closer to her and whispered into her ear "you should say thank you for that."

"Thank you. For not killing me yet," she said wryly.
He laughed. "You're such an unfortunate fellow, you know, Tara. You're so alone, there's no one in the world I could even threaten hurting to get you talking. You have yourself and yourself only. You are all alone"
Tara struggled with his words, but she knew he was right. She really had no one.

"So, I'm left with no choice but to torture you. And I'm going to do it in a way you can never imagine," he said. Then he approached her and touched both sides of her head. Suddenly, the most painful images of her past abuse at the hands of her father began to form in her mind. But it was not quite like she was thinking them as a thought. It was as if she was reliving each experience, feeling each pain again. She let out a heart-rending cry.

Maxwell stopped and whispered into her ear "are you ready to talk? I can do that over and over again, and it will only get worse".

"I did not cheat on you Max. I swear to God," she breathed.

"Keep quiet!" he shouted. "You are lying through your teeth."
She felt him move to touch her again. She could not endure that again.

"The lab, Max, the lab!" she shouted.
He paused. "What about it?"

"I artificially inseminated myself with sperm from an anonymous donor from our sperm bank. I made sure it was one of the anonymous ones so I can never find him. So I never cheated on you. I didn't tell you, yes, but I knew already you can't have children," she said hurriedly.

"You are so pathetic. You couldn't even find a man willing to get you pregnant. You had to resort to your test tubes and frozen cells."

With that, he began to discard his human form before her eyes to transform into a hideous creature. She opened her mouth to scream, but no sound came out.

"I am going to kill you, and offer you to the master," he said in a voice very different from the baritone she was familiar with.

Suddenly, the door flew open and a burst of shots rang out. The hideous creature she was seeing before disappeared and she saw Maxwell crumple over as the bullets hit him. She saw Lamela dash to her side, beginning to untie her, before passing out again.

Maxwell lay frothing on the floor in a pool of his own blood. Lamela left the unconscious Tara's side and knelt by him.

"This was not part of the plan," he said, whizzing as he pronounced each word.

"Oh, it was, Maxwell, it was. I just didn't tell you this part," she responded before shooting him in the head.

THREE

ony swayed and chanted at the top of his voice as Karis led them. If he had told them to slash their wrists at that moment, every single one of them in the warehouse would have gladly done so. Suddenly, as the frenzy seemed to peak, Karis pulled down a lever and the room was filled with smoke. As he inhaled the vapourised drugs, Tony had what he thought was a vision. A being that radiated undiluted power appeared by his side and began to show him things. He felt both at peace and in awe at the same time. It was the most beautiful thing he had ever experienced. Hours later when it was all over, he wanted nothing more than to experience it one more time. He would do anything to see and talk with that being again.

Karis surveyed the result. He was pleased and he was certain Iblis, Nimrod and even Lucifer would also be happy with his work. When Iblis instructed him to have an army of humans who had surrendered their freewill to him without him violating their freewill in the process, it had seemed like a daunting task. But humans are weak. These ones had done just that, and now had companions from the Neatherworld they had freely summoned. They would believe they had had drug induced hallucinations, but they had actually been talking to junior demons.

One was on standby to report something to him now.

"Lord Karis, I think I have happened upon something of great importance amongst one of your followers". It was a hideous looking one-legged fiend. When it appeared to humans that summoned it however, it always took on the form of a very powerful being. It was the one that had answered Tony's call during the chants.

"And what might that be? Since you can now determine what is and what isn't important" Karis asked. One of the bikers sauntered past and hailed Karis on his way out. Now that his high was gone, he couldn't see the spirit that Karis was speaking with.

"Anthony gave me news about a special tattoo he copied from his brother that had caused friction between them because his brother refused to tell him why it was so important. I took a look at it. Crude as his was, it had elements of the fabled Guardians of the Seals tattoo. It is worth investigating if I can get him to summon me again."

"And what are you waiting here for? See, he is leaving. Go with him and watch him. I will arrange a private summon and see what that turns up" Karis responded.

Tony had reached him by now and it was obvious he wanted something. If it was not for the news this demon had given him now, he would have harshly dismissed him. The young man was so needy it was irritating. But now, he turned on the charm.

"When do we do this again, Karis," Tony asked, trying not to betray his desperation. A plan formed in Karis' mind on how to confirm the demon's suspicions. It would rely on the human emotion of love.

"Yes we should. And you know Tony, this was a beginner level experience for the regular members. We're having an elite meet in two days. This is child's play compared to that."

Karis watched him tremble in excitement. Pathetically weak humans who would sell their birthright on a platter of anything. "This level requires doing exactly as you are told. No wavering and no weakness" Karis said.

"Just tell me when. I'll do everything you say," Tony responded.

"Okay then. I'll call you with the details an hour before the event." Karis said.

With that, he turned away from Tony. To the demon he said, "squeal about this to anyone and I will make sure you get Tartarus."

Lamela was tired of waiting for Tara to wake up. She went to open the curtains that ran from the ceiling all the way down and let the sunlight in directly on Tara. In no time, Tara began to stir. She was fully awake a few moments later.

"Did Maxwell make it?" she asked. Above all things, she wanted to know if she was free of him.

"No," Lamela responded.

"And the police? Have they come to ask any questions?" Tara asked further.

Lamela smiled. "They will not be asking any questions."

Tara relaxed. He was gone. Then she remembered something. Lamela anticipated her question and shook her head.

Lamela climbed into the bed beside her and comforted her as Tara broke into quiet sobs. "He killed my baby. That demon killed my baby," Tara wailed. Lamela smiled at how accurate Tara's unwitting description of Maxwell was. "Life has been so cruel to me. Why do bad things keep happening to me?" Tara's voice got louder.

"Life? Life you say?" Lamela was incredulous. She turned Tara around so that their faces were within inches of each other. "You are still refusing to face reality even when it stares you in the face? It is not life that has dealt you cruel blows. No, it is not. It is men. They are the cause of every problem we women have." She got up to pour herself a glass of Whiskey and took a sip before continuing.

"Think about it. Your father. Your husband. Every pain all the women you know have experienced have been caused by the men in their lives. I don't have such problems in my life. Simple reason, I do not have any men in my life. Why do you think everyone at the lab is a woman?"

Tara struggled to form thoughts to refute what Lamela was saying, but every experience from her past fought down those thoughts. She found herself nodding in agreement.

"I have a proposition for you Tara. Because of what you've been through; because of the bond we now share; and because you're my most brilliant researcher."

Tara sat up. "I'm listening."

"Have you ever imagined a world without men and all the problems that they bring into our lives? And by world, I mean that not a single male human remains on this earth."

Tara laughed. "You're joking right?"

"Do I look like I am joking?" Lamela responded. Tara searched her face. She was dead serious.

"Well, the only way that would be possible is if we colonize another planet and somehow forced all the men to move to that planet." Tara said.

"Or we find a way to kill them all" Lamela responded flatly.

"What? That's impossible. And even if it was possible, that would be crazy. And disastrous. Come on Lamela, that would be rather drastic. Surely there are some good men out there."

"Name one you know," Lamela said.

Tara ran a quick scan of her memory. Every man, from her father to her lecturers and her husband had treated her badly because she was a woman. She remained silent.

Lamela scoffed and continued "a few of us who are not afraid to have vision have decided to end the menace of men once and for all. The only way an eradication on a global scale can be achieved is biological. We have hit a brick wall in our research. You can unlock it and create the ultimate man-eradicating biological weapon for us."

"And then what? We all die eventually, unable to reproduce and the human race goes extinct. Then what?" Tara asked.

"Why do you think I've been collecting sperm from anonymous donors into the bank you stole from? That's all we need from the menfolk. We have now collected more than enough to propagate the species without needing men to produce sperm."

"Wow!" Tara exclaimed.

"Yes Tara, we have it all thought out. Now, you need to tell me if you want in or not. If you say no, you can recover from here and go back to your work and forget this conversation happened and I'll forget your husband died yesterday. Mutually assured forgetting. However, if you say yes, then you will be doing humanity the greatest good possible."

Tara's brow wrinkled for some seconds as she weighed the decision. Then she smiled. "Lamela, I have an even better option than the sperm bank. It's something I've worked on for a while now, but just as a side thought: Autogamous reproduction in female humans. We won't need men or even their sperm".

Lamela smiled back, "I take that as a yes?"

"When do I start work?"

Lamela smiled. She had won Iblis. Nimrod would be very happy.

"I have everything you will be needing packed already. Your secret research facility, equipped with the best equipment money can buy is ready. It's a place called The Place."

"You were so sure I would say yes, yeah?" Tara said.

"You bet."

Lamela was preparing to move Tara to The Place when Iblis' call came in.

"We've been summoned by Nimrod with immediate effect. Be here in thirty minutes and be ready to explain yourself," he said curtly.

She was sure Iblis had instigated this meeting to disgrace her. She looked at Tara getting ready and smiled. He wouldn't see her coming.

"I am worried about Anthony," Lex said to his friend as he set the teacup down. They were seated in the portico of Lex's house. One of the benefits of living in the lecturers' quarters in the university was the spacious, well greened compounds.

"What? That he doesn't sleep at home everyday? That strikingly reminds me of you a decade ago. Lex, he's 25. It's normal. You're overthinking, simple." Farida responded.

Lex shook his head. This was different. "I wasn't running around with a motorcycle gang, doing drugs. I need to be firmer with him."

"Look, Lex, try not to make it worse. Pushing him away from you will only make him find more welcome with them."

The sound of a motorcycle pulling up caught their attention. Moments later, Tony was walking towards them.

"Don't" Farida said, anticipating that his friend would want to chastise his brother.

Tony waltzed past them, greeting them cheerily. If he noticed the stern look on his brother's face, he did not give the slightest impression that he did.

Alex was about to say something when Farida signalled to him to hush. "Let's take a stroll," he said.

Silently, they went through the short stone-paved driveway onto the street. They had walked for five minutes before they stopped and sat on a stone bench under a large tree.

"Did I really see what I just thought I saw?" Alex asked rhetorically.

"That's not just a regular demon. So to have it following him must only mean one thing." Farida said.

"It's there with his permission. Freewill. Something must have happened in that his gang." Alex said, holding his head in his hands.

"It's a dangerous situation Lex. You're a Guardian. How do you want to handle this without revealing yourself to your brother? And even if you dispatched this one, its superiors will investigate. We can't afford your identity being revealed to them."

"I know Farida, I know. This boy just had to go and get involved with this. Damn. Where did I go wrong with him?"

"He's an adult Lex. You need to quit blaming yourself for his actions." Farida said.

"So what should I do? How do I begin to solve this problem?" Alex asked.

"We need to tell the others, and inform Gabriel as well." Farida responded.

"No! We can't do that. I'll take care of this, Farida, trust me. This is a family issue," Alex said earnestly.

"Lex, there are rules. You know better than break them," Farida said just as earnestly. He was concerned that his friend's decision making would be clouded by emotion.

"I know the rules Farida. I promise you, whatever I do, I won't break them. But you must promise me that you will keep this between us," Alex said, placing his hand on Farida's shoulder.

Farida knew he had no choice in the matter. He sighed. "I promise."

Lamela got into the meeting room before everyone else. Inside, you could not tell whether it was day or night. They kept the lighting low. Moments after she sat down, the rest of the group came in and took their seats. Iblis came in last, with a pretty human in tow. They needed the human to invoke Nimrod out of her freewill, otherwise he could not enter this realm from the Neatherworld.

Iblis quickly led her in the invocation ritual. There was a crackling sound in the ceiling and suddenly, a thick fog along with a pungent sulphuric smell filled the room. When the fog cleared, Nimrod's wiry form floated above the empty seat Iblis had placed at the head of the table. They all stood and bowed. His single eye surveyed them, noting that they had all gotten weaker with staying in this world. It was good for him. Since the fall, he had risen even as Lucifer's wrath decimated other demons. He didn't exchange greetings with underlings.

"Where is our plan? Have you found a human capable and willing to wipe out the rest of humanity? Or is your team as incompetent as all the other teams. We found you bodies, made sure you were put in influential positions amongst the humans yet you have not justified any of these. You heard what happened to Kurumi's team, didn't you? Lord Lucifer does not like failure. Tartarus awaits you all, should you fail with this simple plan."

Everyone had heard Kurumi's story. None of them in the room wanted that kind of fate dealt to them. Iblis quickly spoke up "Lamela has been working on our best option. We identified her through the agents stationed with her father and saw she was suitable. We then sent in Maxwell to marry her. Lamela is yet to play her part. And I have given her two weeks to do it or be replaced by Batibat here."

"Excuses, excuses. That's all you give. Very soon, you will have to give them before our master. You, Lamela, after thousands of years, you don't know how to work a human any longer?" Nimrod turned his fiery glare on her.

Lamela chuckled inside. She could sense the others laughing and waiting for her to speak and admit failure so Nimrod could pass judgement on her there and then.

"Oh Lord Nimrod. It seems Iblis is not aware of new developments. Maxwell is back in the Neatherwold now. His assignment with the human he speaks of was completed yesterday and she is with me now. Of her freewill, she has not only agreed to the plan, she has even made it better. We were about to leave for the secret lab where she will begin work when I received the summons for this meeting."

"Is that so?" Nimrod asked

"I would not dare lie to you, my lord," she responded.

"Then someone is obviously not on top of things." Nimrod said, turning to Iblis.

"My lord, I can explain…" Iblis responded, stuttering.

"I do not have the time to listen to your ramblings. There is something even more important at hand. The real reason I summoned you all," Nimrod said.

An eerie silence fell upon the room. Their minds raced all over the place attempting to figure out what Nimrod meant. He enjoyed letting them tremble. Without warning, he turned on Karis.

"Did you think I would not find out?" he bellowed.

Karis shrank back and the others heaved a sigh of relief.

"What, lord Nimrod?" he squealed.

"Your little agent attached to the boy told me everything that happened in your meeting yesterday. You have a lead on the Guardians of the Seals and you kept that to yourself? What were you planning? To obtain the seals for yourself and storm heaven, eat of the tree of almightiness and then become our lord?"

Nimrod wrapped his tail around Karis' neck as he spoke, squeezing it harder with each word.

The cursed thing could not keep its mouth shut, Karis thought as he struggled for breath. When it looked like he would pass out, Nimrod unwrapped his tail. He sucked in air, panting.

"My lord, no. I was not thinking any such thing. I only wanted to be sure before reporting the matter. The seals are the biggest treasure we can obtain. I thought it would be better to be sure we had found one of the Guardians. I feared the punishment if I reported finding one and it turned out false. I have a plan"

Nimrod waved in the air and a fiery spear appeared in his hands. "Well, you better start talking now, before I return you to the Neatherworld to face punishment."

Visibly afraid, Karis rushed his words "We want him to be bait, to draw his brother out. His brother loves him dearly and if he is a Guardian, he will attempt to rescue his brother using his powers. That way, we are sure."

"Fool. Then you kill him and steal the seal for yourself." Nimrod responded. Then he turned to Iblis. "All this happened and you did not even know. Yet you want to explain. At least Lamela knows what she is doing. You are hereby demoted from being leader of this team. Lamela takes over immediately. I will be watching you, so obey her."

"But…" Iblis attempted to protest.

"But, what? You prefer to return to the Neatherworld right away?" Nimrod cut in, pointing the spear at Iblis.

Iblis kept quiet. Nimrod continued, "You, Karis, you will continue with your plan but it must happen today. There is no time to be wasted. Call the boy in and give his brother notice he is with you. If he is a Guardian, he must have seen the demon you attached to him already. Lamela, you will go and settle your subject into The Place. She must get this done and quickly. Impress it on her. I will personally be with you Karis. Bring the boy here. Now, get to work!"

Tony sped on his bike to the address Karis had given him. He was elated that the event for the select few of them had come earlier than Karis had told him the night before. He felt special and liked the feeling.

He followed the directions and finally turned into the street he figured was the one Karis described. He didn't have to wonder if he was on the right street. The building stood apart from surrounding buildings on a small elevation at the end of the street. As he approached the gate, it swung open by itself. He was expected. There was no one in sight, but he couldn't shake the feeling of being watch off. He rode down a long driveway. At the end, the familiar sights of a few bikes put him at ease. He pulled up beside the last one and began to walk towards the huge door with a dragon carved along its length. The mouth of the dragon held a thick metal door-knocker. He waited for a few seconds to see if the door would open and then used it to knock. A middle-aged man with sprinklings of gray on his head opened the door.

"Mr. Anthony?" he asked.

"Yes please," Tony responded.

The man stepped aside and he entered a large room dominated by a large bookshelf and a huge chandelier in the ceiling. The man walked up to the bookshelf and touched some invisible button. The shelf slid aside to reveal a large room, lit with torches and dominated by a marble altar. Five people were seated around the altar in grey hooded robes. One of them stood up and lifted the hood and smiled. Tony recognized him immediately. "Welcome to the gathering of elders," Karis said to Tony.

Farida returned to the house with Lex to take his car. Lex had agreed to discretely handle the demon tagging along with Tony and then impress upon his brother the need to go through the wicket gate. They were at the gate when they saw three bikers approaching at top speed. Lex's eyes darted quickly to where Tony's bike should be. It wasn't there. He looked at Farida. It was clear they were seeing the same thing. As the bikes stopped in front of them, the hideous forms housed by the human shells were evident to them. Not one of the riders was a mere human.

"We know you can see who we really are, but what will you do about it?" the one who appeared to be their leader said.

"Nothing! Always hiding," the other two chorused.

"What do you want?" Lex asked coolly. He did not understand the game they were playing but he was not ready to give away the fact that he could see them as they really were.

"You still choose to act ignorant? Are you not a Guardian of the Seal?" the leader said.

Farida flinched for a moment. Did they know for certain? Had Lex told his brother who told his friends? No, he reasoned. Lex would not do such a stupid thing. These ones were guessing.

"What is that? Guardian? Seal?" Farida responded.

"Of course you won't know anything about that. But your friend her does and he will tell us." The biker leader said, with a wicked smile on his face. But that confirmed to Farida that they didn't know anything. Lex must have figured that out too because he responded "I do not know what you are talking about. Your friend is not home. Now you will leave or I will call the school authorities to report that you are constituting a nuisance."

He handed a tablet device to Lex. "We have your brother with us. Many, more powerful than us are with him there. He is there of his own freewill, so no rules are being broken. He will die. There are only two ways you can save him: Either by bringing a small army - which you do not have - to fight your way in, or you use your powers as a Guardian of the Seal. If you don't, your brother's blood will be on your hands. You have exactly an hour from now."

Before Lex could say anything, they jumped on their bikes and sped off. He looked into the tab. It was live-streaming a ceremony from a room with a marble altar. There were six people in the room. Five were in grey robes. The last was wearing a jacket Lex could not miss anywhere. He had bought it for Tony along with his first bike. As if on cue, Tony turned around and looked into the camera. The eyes that Lex saw looked dead already.

Farida placed a hand on his shoulder. "Now, we must tell the others." Lex nodded his head in agreement.

FOUR

"You seem very pleased with yourself", Tara said to Lamela as they rode in the back of her bulletproof sedan on the way to The Place.

Lamela smiled. Of course she was. She had outfoxed Iblis finally, had Tara where she needed her, saved her own skin from punishment in the Neatherworld, gotten rid of Maxwell and topped it all with a promotion. To Tara, she said "I'm simply pleased to have helped another woman see the light".

"You know, I used to wonder why my mother never left my father in spite of how bad he treated her. And then why she prevented me from leaving home when I tried to. I despised her. Yet I became like her, staying on, no matter how horribly Maxwell treated me." Tara responded.

"No, you are nothing like her. Look at you. You survived him and are taking action to rid the world of their evil. You, my dear, are as far from your mother as can be."

"I survived thanks to you, Lamela. And even this chance to do something about men, it is you that is giving it to me. I'm very indebted to you."

Lamela looked up. She could see the shape of the demon Nimrod had assigned to follow and monitor them hovering above the car. This conversation was for its benefit. It would later report to Nimrod that the woman was totally under her control and it was out of her own freewill.
They continued the rest of the drive in silence. Tara noted that the compound felt like a maximum security prison. Lamela read her mind.

"For the sensitivity of the work we do here, security is of the utmost importance," she explained and Tara nodded. They walked past the first set of buildings to a small one in the back. Lamela led her in. "Your work is even more sensitive. Few people will have clearance to the section you'll be working."

With that, she placed her finger on a scanner and the wall at the back opened into a bigger room. It contained some of the most advanced equipment Tara had ever seen. "This is your lab," she announced.

A small-framed lady came out from behind a huge microscope. Lamela greeted her and then turned to Tara. "Thelma here is your assistant. She will show you around and help you to settle in. I need to run now. If you need anything, call me."

Tara gave Lamela a big hug. "Thank you once again Lamela. For everything."

Tony was now wearing a hooded robe like the rest of the people in the room. Like the night before, the room was filled with the vapour of the drug; and as he inhaled, the high he had craved so long returned. Suddenly, he saw a light again and his companion appeared. This time, it touched his forehead and he felt a rapture greater than anything he had ever felt burst through his veins.

"Karis has told you there is someone higher than me. I am unworthy to even unbuckle his sandals," it told him. Tony muttered a weak yes.

"Well, to see him, you must be ready to sacrifice. The law of this level is written in blood. In sacrificing, you might be transformed. Observe," it said and pointed to Karis.

As Nimrod had instructed, Karis knew his time on the earth was done. In obeying Nimrod and following the plan, he was at least guaranteed that he would receive no punishment when he returned to the Neatherworld. On cue of the demon that was speaking to Tony now, he picked up the white marble knife on the altar. He felt with his spirit to be sure the rest were ready. He needed them to make sure his disappearance was of light and not his true being when he left his body. It was not beyond them to withhold their help out of spite just to make him fail. Satisfied, he plunged the knife into his own heart.

Across the room, Tony watched in amazement as Karis stabbed himself and fell on the table lifeless. But even as he touched the table, he saw a being emerge from the body - one lovelier than his own companion. The new Karis emanated light and power, and his clothes had been transformed into radiant armor. He held a glowing sword in hand, and white wings unfurled on his back. He glanced in Tony's direction and a wave of beautiful emotions like nothing he had ever felt before washed over Tony. He heard Karis' voice as if coming from within. "This is what you can become. If you are willing to make the sacrifice," then he rose into the ceiling and was gone.

Karis rose out of the building to meet Nimrod.

"Are you not done playing angel of light?" Nimrod asked

Instantly, Karis' lovely form disappeared. In its place, a man-sized spider stood.

"Better. Your time here is done. Wait for me before going to report to Lucifer on your return. You know better than to try to double-cross me and disobey. Be gone."

With that, Karis vanished, leaving only wisps of smoke where he had been.

"Now, let us see if you are right and that one is truly a Guardian".

Lex had never made a decision that everything in him kicked against like the one he just made. The argument had been heated, with the other two Benzahr and Eldad insisting he protect the secret of the seals. Only Farida was determined to damn the consequences and use their powers to rescue the boy. "If my only brother was held by demons, I would go in with blazing swords and destroy everything that stood in the way of his rescue."

"And jeopardize the whole world in the process by walking into an obvious trap?" Benzahr had asked.

"What then is the use of our power if we cannot use it in great need like this? What is the purpose of power?" Farida quipped.

"With great power, comes great responsibility," Eldad said, reminding them all of Gabriel.

"If only Gabriel was here, he would know what to do," Farida said. They had projected the tab onto a bigger screen and watched as one of the hooded people in the room stabbed himself in the chest.

They all looked to Lex. He had not said anything as they went back and forth. Lex sensed that whatever he said would carry the day. He cleared his throat.

"A Guardian must weigh the cost of his actions with eternity in view," he said, reminding them what Gabriel told him on the day the seal had chosen him. He must have certainly told them the same. "There was nothing special about me. I was an orphan who had nothing. I was not particularly pious or strong. Yet the seal chose me at the end of a long line of Guardians from the patriarch Jacob himself. I didn't think I was worthy and still don't think I am. But Gabriel told me that the seals never made mistakes. Now, my resolve is being tested. I will not bring the apocalypse on all because of one. I will do what all ordinary men would do."

Farida opened his mouth to protest, but Lex raised a hand to silence him. "My mind is made up. I will carry my own cross."

With that, he called the police. On the screen, Tony walked to the marble altar and picked up the knife. Farida shook his head and looked away from the screen. If they would use their powers, they would be there in the blink of an eye.

Nimrod watched as the two police cars pulled up to the building. They would find nothing, not even a body in the building. The tablet Lex had been given would have nothing on it. But the man had called the police. No flash, no swords, no seals. This had been a waste of his time. This Lex was no Guardian. He made a mental note to punish the demon that set him on the path as he descended into the fiery Neatherworld that he called home. Lamela had to succeed with the woman.

FIVE

ara jumped up suddenly from her sleep. Her face was covered in sweat. These dreams were becoming a part of her life now. The only thing the dreams had in common was that they were all gory, bloody and filled with the dark twisted shapes of the beings that really ran The Place. She remembered thinking how similar to a maximum security prison The Place looked on her first day. That thought had been clairvoyant; it was now her prison. She had been here for a little over two years. The first two years had been great. She got every single thing she asked for to carry out her work. Lamela had been sweet, celebrating every progress she made, no matter how small. It was the scientist's dream. She had even forgotten about Maxwell. Until that day. Everything had become a nightmare on that day, a few months ago, when Lamela found out she had used herself as a test successfully for her autogamous reproduction research. She shuddered at the memory of that day when she found out who, no, what Lamela really was. She could not continue living this way any longer. Today, she was going to end the nightmare one way or the other. As if on cue, she heard the click-clack of heels in the hallway. Adrenaline rushed through her in an instant, and the sleep cleared fully from her eyes. It was now or never. She had to escape now, or those dark dreams would come true. She had to do it for her baby.

The door opened. A nurse entered the room. Tara rose on her bed and calmed her nerves as the nurse approached. Quickly, in a sudden, swift motion, she hit the nurse at the two points she had rehearsed. Then she picked up the stun gun that fell from the nurse's hands. What she had just done would buy her only about twenty minutes, but she would take the chance. Hurriedly, she changed into the nurse's clothes and rushed out of the cell.

"Calm down Tara," she muttered to herself. She needed to be discreet. The nurse would never rush.

As she approached the gates of The Place minutes later, she tried to steady herself to a regular walking pace. So far, she had been able to go through the two security checks undiscovered. She knew it was only a matter of time before someone discovered the stunned nurse in her room. And once that happened, the hunt for her would begin in earnest. The plan had begun to form in her mind from the first day she saw her new nurse. Thelma, her former assistant had been her first nurse. One day, Thelma did not show up. Tara had asked the new nurse what happened, but got no answers. This new nurse was about Tara's size, a pretty young lady. She was obviously inexperienced. She did not exercise the degree of care Thelma did and turned her back on Tara while serving her food and dropping supplies for the day. It was what proved providential for Tara.

The nurses were the only people that Tara was allowed contact with, once in the morning and once in the evening. This had been her only interaction with humans in the four months. Most of the regular workers did not even know that the underground section where she had worked existed. It was why her plan had worked so far. No one recognized her.

She had run the whole of her escape plan in her mind until she knew every option, every possibility and she knew this scenario was her only chance of success. And even then, it was just a chance. Something could go wrong, and her plan could come tumbling down like a pack of cards. Yet, she had to try; if she didn't, her life's work would be lost. She hoped that not much had changed in the layout of The Place since her incarceration. She relied on her memory to plot her escape. So far, everything had checked out as she had pictured it in her head. But it had taken longer than she had estimated to clear the first two checkpoints.

She was short on time, both to escape and with regards to her condition. Her pregnancy was just entering the second trimester and so it wasn't showing yet. The moment her tummy began to show off her pregnancy, she knew she would be unable to pull off any sort of escape. Her escape depended on her being able to pass herself off as one of the nurses. So when the chance presented itself to her today, she was ready. As usual, the nurse had turned her back. She had not seen Tara coming. Tara's hit was precisely at the point that would cut off the nurse's air supply for long enough till she landed the second hit on the spot on the nurse's temple that sent her to sleep without as much as a gasp.

Now, Tara trudged on in the military style nurse uniform under the moonlight. She had met none of the workers in the general lab but the guards at the checkpoints all through her escape. The running of The Place was so organised that the people had minimal contact with one another and when they did have contact, they tended to avoid conversation. Everyone did their jobs and followed procedure. Deviation from procedure would cause one to stick out like a sore thumb and here, no one wanted that. The thought of what she would do once she got out through the gates crossed her mind, but she forced that thought out of her head as quickly as it came in. If she allowed it stay for too long, she would definitely lose her nerve and would be discovered. When she reached that bridge, she would find a way to cross it. She would rather sink at the bridge than not even get there at all.

She got to the gatehouse and pressed the buzzer that would bring the guard to the door. The gatehouse was a small, flat-topped concrete building that stood flushed into the fence right beside the huge main gate. A shuffling of feet from inside told her that someone was getting up and moving towards the door. She steeled her nerves as the sound of the rubber boots on the tiled floor stopped. There was a short click and the hydraulics of the lock whizzed to open the door.

A guard literally filled the doorway when the door finally opened, his khaki uniform crisp from the starching and ironing. He looked stern as he arched his eyebrows while questioning her reason for wanting to leave the facility. She knew if she showed any timidity here, she would raise his suspicion. And she didn't need him to keep her for any moment longer than necessary. Time was not on her side.

Back in the cell, the nurse stirred. Lamela had assigned her to watch this prisoner with stern warnings about the punishment that would befall her if anything went wrong. Now, she had managed to lose Tara. She howled, a blood-curdling sound that came from the demon inside the human form. She cursed the weak nature she was constrained to bear in this human form and longed to be in her demon form, so she could fly through the walls and bring a thousand tortures on Tara. She resorted to using her two-way radio. She wanted to call the gatehouse first, so they could seal the perimeter. She would call Lamela after that. She howled one more time in dread of the suffering and punishment that awaited her for this error. She pressed the radio key she needed. No tone. It was then she realised her radio batteries had been taken out.

"Cursed human!" she swore. She quickly let herself out of the cell, not bothered that she was naked, and raced towards the control room. She desperately needed to make that call.

Tara shifted uncomfortably from one foot to the other. If the guard noticed her discomfort, he did not show it. Every extra second brought detection closer. She cleared the lump in her throat and looked straight at him.

"I have an Alpha Code delivery to make."

The guard flinched for a moment, trying to decide whether to probe further or not. She did not volunteer any further information to him. If indeed she had an Alpha Code delivery, then she didn't need to explain herself further. Just getting through the first two levels also gave credence to her claims. The guard went back in wordlessly for what was a few seconds but seemed like an endless wait to Tara. The shadows seemed to be coming for her from every corner and an owl she couldn't see hooted somewhere in the woods. Everything had a sinister shade to it. She put her hand in her pocket and fiddled with the object she had carefully concealed there, as if to find comfort in its icy cold body. The way it stung her fingers gave her the presence of mind she needed.

Just when she was beginning to wonder if she had been caught, the huge gates parted ways and freedom stared her in the face. She hesitated for a few moments as the reality of the prospect sank in. The air that blew in from the other side seemed cleaner, less repressive. The grass indeed looked greener on that side of the fence. Then the sirens blared, the sound stinging her like a thousand angry bees and lifting her out of her thoughts. From within the gatehouse, she could hear raised voices. Someone had alerted the guards! The gates began to close together and she felt a panic begin to rise from within her belly. She fought the feeling down and with all that was left in her, lunged forward and landed on the paved road outside just as the gates snapped shut. Quickly, she picked herself up and looked around. The road stretched for as long as she could see under the moonlight. There was a vast field of tall grass on each side, dotted here and there by trees. She recalled that somewhere further down the road, it branched into two roads. The one to the left was tarred, but taking the road led straight back to The Place. The way out was the least likely of the two – the bumpy, dusty road. From where she stood, she could see the gatehouse and the hefty guard who had let her out. Another even heftier one accompanied him. They were fast approaching her, moving with a speed that was unbelievable for their size. She patiently waited for them to be within good proximity. Then her hands went in and out of her pocket in a flash. She produced the tranquilizer gun she had taken from her nurse. Two well-placed shots and the men stopped in their tracks and went to ground. She had developed the tranquilizing agent and she knew its effect would be instant. She did not wait for them to hit the ground before she turned and began to run. She had bought herself valuable time before they came after her again in full force. She had to be at that road fork before they caught up with her.

She had been running under the moonlight for a couple of minutes when it began to dawn on her that she had overestimated how strong she was. The months of inactivity in her cell had left her muscles weak. Being months pregnant did nothing to help her endurance either. Fatigue was already setting in and her pace was beginning to slow. She had started to hear the sounds of her pursuers and as the seconds went by, the barks of the security dogs and the voices of the people were getting louder. Soon, she would begin to see the lights from their torches. She could see the tarred road ahead, but it seemed that with each step she took now, someone was adding lead weights to her feet. Her legs were feeling heavier and heavier. Her vision was beginning to get blurry. Then, without announcement, her legs finally gave way beneath her. She willed herself to get up, but her body refused to respond. With a sigh, she shut her eyes as she resigned herself to her fate. At least she had tried.

Suddenly, she felt a warmth engulf her. It seemed to start from a core inside her and spread out from there to her finger and toe tips and then beyond. She felt herself leave the ground. Someone was picking her up, but rather than the rough manner in which she had expected her pursuers to act, this person carried her so gently it felt as though she was floating. She tried to open her eyes to see who it was, but all she saw was swirling patterns. Finally, through the haze, she saw the side view of a man's face. And he was not wearing the khaki of the guards from The Place. Then she lost consciousness.

Lamela was reclining before her fireplace when she got the news of Tara's escape. She knew this was a big disaster. But she was a survivor. She would salvage this before ...

The summon from the Neatherwold interrupted her thoughts. Lucifer himself had issued the order. The program had been cancelled and they had failed their Lord. It was game-over for her and The Place. She had always prepared for a time like this, but had hoped it would never come. She walked to her table and pressed a button. On the screen above, she watched as the explosions began to go off. First, in The Place. Then in her lab, with all the cancer stem cell samples and the sperm samples collected. If she was going down, she might as well take them with her.

As she plunged the marble knife into her breast, she knew that it was all over for her, both in this world, and in the one she was going back to. The explosion of her apartment hit as her body hit the floor.

Lucifer was outraged. He hated failure in any magnitude and severely punished any in his fold that failed him. Worse than failure, he hated the fact that everyone thought something other than their own ineptitude was responsible for their failure. They always had an "if only" or "it was because" to explain their failures. The billows of his smoky kingdom rose all around him, the rage of the fire pits struggling to match his.

In all this time, the earth had changed much. A lot of the green had been replaced by things that men had built. But Neatherworld remained the same burning place, the perpetual stench of decay in its air. Before Lucifer's throne stood five trembling demons waiting to know their fate. They had brought the news of the woman's escape to him. Another set of failures. Nimrod stood beside Lucifer's throne, his twisted, wiry form a contrast to his master's hulking form. He had clawed his way up from being a lowly demon to becoming the right hand demon of the demon lord himself. Every demon, whether in Neatherworld or working in the earth realm, knew better than to get into his bad books. Over the course of time, he had built an army of loyal followers by skilfully interceding on their behalf when it would have been certain that Lucifer would have sentenced them to Tartarus. In that position, he heard most things before they came to Lucifer's hearing. And he used that prior knowledge to his advantage many times. He never promised anything though. Lucifer was too unpredictable and Nimrod knew that even his own position was not as secure as he made the other demons believe.

Lucifer bellowed and the whole place shook at his voice. "How could a single, pregnant woman escape from all of you and your stupid humans? She was on foot! She cannot fly! She cannot disappear! So, how?"

The demons were too frightened to speak. "Which one is your leader?" he bellowed. Lamela timidly stepped forward. Her eni form was that of what men called a basilisk.

"You could not keep the woman, you fiend?"

"My lord Lucifer, it was not my fault. It was…"

"Mine? Beelzebub!" Lucifer called.

A buzz like a thousand bees filled his throne-room and a giant fly-like demon appeared.

"Take that piece of filth away," Lucifer ordered. Immediately, Beelzebub picked Lamela up with one of its legs and took her away.

"Now, which of you want to tell me what happened?" Lucifer turned to the four remaining demons.

Nimrod spoke up from behind Lucifer. "She must have had help. Was there a traitor amongst your humans? Or was she helped by someone from outside the facility?"

One of the demons took the cue and quickly answered. "We were upon her but lost her when a great light came from above. It blinded and stunned all of us. By the time we recovered, she was gone and…"

"Shut up!" Lucifer retorted angrily. "You incompetent vermin! You fabricate fantasies off the top of either of your heads to excuse your incompetence."

Nimrod moved quickly again to salvage the situation. Maybe it would be a good idea to steer this conversation himself rather than let those wretches practically open the gates of Tartarus with their own words, he thought.

"My lord," he began, his voice smooth as silk as Lucifer turned his attention towards him. "While these worms have been more than incompetent and deserve to be punished, it might be a good idea to take a closer look at their story. It seems that the human woman was indeed helped from outside." Nimrod paused to observe his master's reaction to this, so he could know whether to retreat or proceed. Lucifer waved his hand as to signal that he was listening and Nimrod could continue his monologue.

"When I debriefed them, they described the light that incapacitated them as they closed in on the woman. Their description has led me to believe that if these vermin are telling the truth, the help the woman received was not just from outside; it was from above. The enemy is on the move again." Nimrod wanted to continue, but something in the slight movement of Lucifer's eyes told him to stop. He was rolling it in his mind. After a short pause, Lucifer spoke. "We need to confirm this. If indeed it is true, then the woman has become significantly more important." He turned to the demons before him. "You get out of my sight now!" Then he turned to Nimrod. "Get the Seers to the location of her escape. If indeed there was anything divine that used its powers there, I need this confirmed quickly." With that, he waved his scaly arm to dismiss his lieutenant and Nimrod slithered away. Iblis and his cohorts had been saved.

Tara opened her eyes and the rest of her senses along with them. Sunlight streaked into the room from a high window and birdsong from outside came into her ears as the sleep cleared from her eyes. The bed she lay in was a large one, and she felt the softness of the mattress, something she had become unfamiliar with. She was dressed in a free-flowing silk gown with lace trimmings at the end. Her head was throbbing and when she tried to turn around so she could take in the details of where she was, pain shot through her being like a lightning bolt.

Then it all came rushing back. The Place. Lamela. Her escape. The pursuit and how she had almost been caught. And then someone helped her. Now she wondered who that someone could be. What did the person want? What was the person even doing around The Place at that time and how had he dealt with her pursuers?

"Ha!" she groaned. "Even thinking makes me want to cut this head off." Her voice was surprisingly clear.

"There are many who would love nothing more to happen," came a deep, rich male voice from somewhere she guessed was the door of the room. She tried to sit up to see who it was, and the hammer inside her head hit again. She fell back into the bed.

"I wouldn't do that if I were you," the voice said. "Just lie down and be still. You've been out for two whole days. You probably won't be able to sit up for another day."

By now, the man had covered the distance between where he was and Tara's bed. He sat at the edge of the bed to her left. She turned her head left to get a glimpse of his face. She found herself looking into piercing brown eyes that seemed to look into her soul. From what she could see of his upper body, she guessed he was a tall and well-proportioned man. He had a kind of face that glowed when he smiled and became very stern when he became serious, and could move from smiling to being serious in an instant. Now he switched from the smiling face he had when entering the room into the serious face, framing his hairless face in his left palm.

"The situation is a serious one," he said. "There are many who seek you and the child you carry, but they all come from one source. The child must survive. Everything will depend on it." He said that in a matter-of-fact manner that made her believe him.

"But who are you?" she asked. "You appear from nowhere, save me from people we should not have been able to get away from… how did you even know I was pregnant? How could everything, whatever that means, depend on the experiment in my womb?"

"Questions, questions, questions," he responded, his face turning tender. "We ask so many of those and then get the answers and have a ton more. Then the question we asked initially doesn't help us again, it only confuses us. Sometimes, we don't need to know, we need to just trust." Then he bent close enough for her to see his eyes clearly and whispered, "Trust me."

It was as if he had said magic words. A part of her still tried to tell her she hated all men and she wanted to kill them all. But in some inexplicable way, she found that her heart seemed to begin to trust him of its own volition. She fell back into a deep, peaceful sleep.

Gabriel lingered for a while, watching over the frail woman in the bed. He had watched her through the years as she went through the pain of her childhood and how she had allowed the pain to direct her towards the choices she had made, rather than take all the opportunities to make the ones that would lift her out of the dark places. But he had never intervened directly, until today. The instruction had been clear when it came to him - save her and preserve the child. He had gladly moved in. He did not still fully understand why an archangel of his level was assigned to this human woman and her child. But whatever it was, he knew it had to be big. Over the years, he had become somewhat attached to her. He adjusted the covers on Tara and then turned to leave the room. He would protect her.

Lucifer could not believe what he was seeing. The Seers had brought back evidence that indeed there had been a divine intervention in the woman's case. And it had not been the rank and file of Heaven that had been sent. It was someone very powerful. He had attached some importance to her before, as one of the many plans Nimrod had running to destroy the world. But with this development, he knew that the woman held significant importance greater than all that. Forces of the level that had been dispatched to save her did not leave Heaven except there was a real threat to someone really important.

He had dispatched his best seeking demons to go and scour for her everywhere on the earth, but it was as if she had vanished from the face of the earth. She was nowhere to be found. She was definitely being hidden by someone very powerful. But he would be patient. He had learnt over thousands of years that all he needed to do in most cases was wait for long enough. She was human. Even if she had the most powerful angel watching over her, she would slip up. Humans always did.

Gabriel held the baby girl wrapped in a chequered shawl in his arms. The four months that had led up to her birth and eventually her birth had been uneventful for one so important. No stars aligning, no comet falling, no earthquakes or thunderstorms. Not even one flash of lightning. It was just a regular sunny day in a house on a hill. He smiled at the irony of it. The last few months had been challenging, and Lucifer's seekers had come close twice. But he had been able to successfully hide Tara from them. He knew his time here was limited. He went into the room where Tara sat on the bed. She had gradually recovered from her incarceration at The Place and as the time had gone by, she had practically taken charge of taking care of the house, even in the advanced stages of her pregnancy. But more importantly, Gabriel had helped her heal a deeper wound. Gradually, she had dropped the toxic ideas she had been filled with about men as he showed her what a real man should be. And in doing so, she had become a more complete woman. She was a strong one, this woman. Now, she knew the hiding place inside out and it could be rightly called her new home.

Gabriel sat by her on the bed as she took her baby from him. "What will you call her?" he asked.

"I've been thinking… you have been everything the man of the house would have been if I had a husband. Not that I need one, but I guess you know what I mean. I want you to name the child."

Gabriel smiled. He touched the baby's head. "We will call her Imani. The world will need her to believe and have faith at some point. She will struggle to believe, but when she finally does, her destiny will be made manifest."

"Imani," Tara said, and rolled the name over on her tongue. She liked the sound of it. The child that bore the name looked as exotic as the name sounded. Her hair was jet black and thick, her complexion olive-coloured, a tone darker than Tara's, even as a baby. She had big, full eyes that seemed to question everything they were fixed on. Tara rocked her. Imani. Her own. In those moments, Imani was just her child. All that Gabriel was saying about the world needing her for something didn't register. She was holding her child, and she would die first before any harm came to her.

It was as if Gabriel heard her thoughts. "I know you love her more than the world and would do all in your power to keep her safe," he said. "I wish

I could stay with you for longer, but my time here is indeed up."

As he spoke and Tara watched on, a soft light began to engulf him, and then the same warmth that had engulfed her on the night she escaped filled her whole being again. She began to hear Gabriel's voice, not with her ears anymore, but with her being as a whole. When she looked up again, there was only a lingering light where he had stood. Her heart did a little lurch as he disappeared. She thought she would feel alone, but strangely, she didn't. Somehow, she knew they would be okay, her and Imani.

Six

mani waited for her chauffeur to open the door before she stepped out of her multipurpose vehicle. She was one of the elite who could afford flying cars and she intended to enjoy that status to the fullest. The chauffeur could have opened her door from his seat with the press of a button, but she would rather he did it the old-fashioned way of coming down to open for her. Such subtle display of power was a natural part of her branding and image, and she played well on it. When the door opened, she stepped confidently out onto the steps that led to the reception of the fourteen-storey building that housed the office of her powerful media organisation, Direct Buzz.

At twenty-eight, she was already a phenomenal success. She had latched on to a patent her researcher mother had filed to interface human neural networks with the internet. She had developed this when everyone was still skeptical about trying such bold new things and it had paid off. Now, people did not need to carry external devices to search the internet, make calls and access all data exchange types of services. They could interface their thoughts directly with these networks using her device. And that had opened a whole new world for how people accessed and used information. All this put her at the forefront of this world. Now, she sat atop the greatest media organisation in the world. So far, the greatest threat to her empire had been governments trying to interfere by attempting to use Direct Buzz as a monitoring tool for their people. Imani had succeeded in dealing with this threat. What those government clowns did not understand was that people only accepted Direct Buzz Interfacers because they trusted that it was not being used to monitor them. Break this trust and the business would crumble.

As she waited for the elevator to come down, a call came through to her Interfacer. She had one of the more recent models and it allowed her quickly run a number through her call log before picking it. It was that guy again. He had been calling her religiously for a month now. She had wondered how he got her direct Interfacer number, since she did not exactly have it listed on the net. She had given him the cold shoulder at first, but he had been persistent. With time, she began to enjoy conversations with him. They had not yet met physically, but she had to admit to herself that she had grown fond of him. Now, she actually looked forward to his calls. She had not dated for most of her life, except for a few high profile relationships her publicist had advised her to have, for the cameras. She had been too busy building her company and considered men a distraction. But this one had patiently worked his way past her defences, even if she had not let him in on that fact. She had refused to see him because she didn't want the magic to end. She feared that what made this special would go away once she saw him. She answered the Interfacer as she got on the elevator.

"And you have yourself a fantastic day, ok?" Lucan cooed as he rounded off the call.

He wondered when Imani would finally let go and let him have his way with her. She still hadn't made her mind up about seeing him. Any other person would have become exasperated after the first two calls, but not Lucan. He had kept at it, calling her at precise times daily, until her ice slowly thawed. He felt the ice would soon totally melt and she would be his. He had a thing for ice princesses, and she was the classic one. The more he heard about her, the more intrigued he had become. As they talked, it had grown from mere intrigue to something more, and although he didn't admit it to himself yet, he was falling in love.

He had never been one to shy away from challenges, so the more difficult she was, the more his desire for her grew.

"Well well, she's worth the wait," he mumbled to himself. He stood up from his reclining chair and looked at himself in the mirror. The figure that stared back at him was a pleasant one. His face had little hair and the lack of clutter made his eyes the most prominent features of his face. His eyes were deep, brooding and mysterious. Most people said he said more with his eyes than he did with his mouth. His whole being had a good symmetry and his figure was built for strength. Strong arms, broad chest and feet that seemed to plant themselves into the ground when he stood He had never been one to like anyone telling him what to do and that had influenced his choice of profession. He was a writer and with two bestselling books that had been adapted into Direct Interfacer movies, he didn't need to work at the frenetic pace and within the defined confines of those around him. He took his time to do everything; most people would describe him as laid-back. But Lucan would prefer to describe himself as having a hint of genius. He knew how to make accomplishing difficult tasks look easy and effortless. He liked his life the way it was.

He went into the kitchen to fix breakfast.

Lucifer was addressing the general assembly of the demon lords. It was a leap year and the time for The Bringing. All his major lieutenants were gathered. There was Lilith, the seductress who spawned lust amongst men. There was four-faced Abadon, the keeper of his gates, who could see simultaneously in all the four directions of the wind. Apollyon, the destroyer, was here too. He was in charge of creating wars and pestilence amongst men. Apollyon's lieutenant, Beelzebub, in the form of a huge housefly, buzzed his wings as he perched by Apollyon's side. Beelzebub was strong enough to be a lieutenant in his own right, but he unusually remained loyal to Apollyon. Mantov, the head troll was also present. So was Nimrod, who took the prime position right beside Lucifer. Green envy was in the eyes of all the other demon lords, but they all knew that Nimrod was the demon lord with the most power now. Even amongst their ranks, there were many whose real allegiance was with Nimrod, because he had saved them from certain destruction.

This was a gathering that was held together only by their common fear of their master. The reason for this gathering was to present their candidates for The Bringing. Already, Mantov and Lilith's candidates had been discussed and struck out.

Apollyon addressed the gathering in his grating voice. "I am presenting Bukar Uri." As he spoke, pictures of a young man in military uniform formed in a haze.

"He is the foremost military strategist on the earth right now," Apollyon continued. "He believes there is no Wicket Gate, no Heaven, and no life after his earth existence. He is secretly working to form an alliance where the military will take over in half the states of the world and he'll turn them all into a police state. Imagine the amount of damage that could be done to the world through this man."

"If on his own he could do that much damage, why do we want to use him as the sacrifice at The Bringing to the great Lucifer?" Lilith asked.

Mantov growled in agreement, nodding his huge head.

"Don't be a sore loser, little Lilith," Apollyon spat, his thick leathery wings rubbing against each other, producing an unpleasant scratching sound. He turned his attention back at Lucifer. "My lord, Bukar is the candidate," he restated. "With the influence he has gathered and the plans he has laid down, I am convinced that if he is sacrificed and Beelzebud took his body and his place, those plans could be actualised faster and we could have another world scale war. It would be a bloodbath that would dwarf any other before it."

Nimrod watched the proceedings. He realised why he was the favoured one of Lucifer. These other demons pre-empted Lucifer and presented their thoughts to him as their own. He knew without thinking much that Lucifer would not accept Apollyon's candidate.

When Lucifer eventually spoke, his voice was laced with boredom. "If your candidate has done so well on his own, we will leave him to continue. One of your stronger demons will take the place of one of the men in his inner circle and observe and report things from there."

Nimrod then took a low bow. "If I may speak, my lord," he asked.

"Speak Nimrod and leave out the drama," Lucifer grunted.

The others murmured their approval of Lucifer's reproach of Nimrod.

Nimrod continued, ignoring them. "A young woman has created the best platform to get into the minds of these humans. That I believe is the key we have been looking for. For as a man thinks in his heart, so is he. The young woman fits the mould- youthful, high achiever, self-believer. We could use the Most Influential Tomorrow Leader award as a front. When she is sacrificed, my lord can select a capable demon to take her place. By so doing, my lord will have a great tool in his possession to do his bidding."

Abadon cut in with a face that looked coolly at Nimrod, his other three faces directed towards his fellow lords. "Nimrod, Nimrod, Nimrod. Who would think of such a lily-livered plan but you?"

"Nimrod has gone very soft," Apollyon added, "if that is the best he can come up with."

Nimrod wasn't bothered. They could all run their mouths, but only one opinion mattered here, and that was the one he waited to hear. He would not come down to their bickering level to explain or defend his suggestion.

Lucifer leaned forward in his throne and with that gesture all the demon lords fell silent. "You have forgotten the goal," he said sternly. "The final aim is to leave this cursed place and return to our former estates! There is only one portal into heaven and this much we know – there are four guardians that each hold one seal and a keystone is held by another. But you incompetent clowns have been unable to find the guardians or the seals or the keystone for millennia. The Bringing is a mere distraction to keep me amused until you discover how we can get into heaven. The one that makes this discovery will share of the fruit of the Tree of Almightiness with me. Do you all lack ambition such that none of you can bring me any news on the seals? I am surrounded by jabbering buffoons!"

By now a great crackling had begun all around as if in response to Lucifer's anger at his lieutenants. For a moment, palpable fear ran through all of them. They thought it was the crackle of Tartarus' gates. When Lucifer stood up from his throne, they were sure it was over for them. He looked from one to the other, and when his eyes lingered on any of them, it seemed he would pass judgment. But he simply continued talking. "We will take Nimrod's plan. Go and prepare your minions for the event. I will make a personal appearance at the sacrifice of the chosen one. Does she have a name, Nimrod?"

"Imani, my lord, Imani."

"Imani," Lucifer rolled the name on his tongue. "Then Imani it will be." With that, he vanished in a puff of smoke, leaving his lieutenants.

"I win again, as always," Nimrod said to the spirits of all five lords at once. Then he left too.

Three figures gathered around the bed in the dimly lit room in the small brick bungalow. The conversation was light and their laughter was easy, a little too easy. The reason lay in the bed before them - Farida. Their friend and companion of many years was dying. Stripped to the waist, an intricately woven tattoo stood out on his left breast. His red hair, now pale from stress his body had gone through, stood out spiky on his head. The three figures recounted stories of their years together and laughed heartily. They held hands and sang old hymns. Then they noticed that the tattoos on Farida's chest began to glow. They all stopped singing. It was only then that they realised that Farida had stopped singing for some time. He had stopped breathing, his lips arched as if to form a word of the song he was singing. Line by line, the tattoo began to rise out of his skin like beads of bright white light, until it formed into a wavy, finger length item that lay on his chest. In the dimness of the room, it gave out a cool light, and looked like solidified flowing water. Heads bowed, the three men finished the hymn they had been singing.

Hevenu Shalom, Aleichem

Hevenu Shalom, Aleichem

Hevenu Shalom, Shalom, Shalom Aleichem

Hevenu Shalom… Aleichem.

Gabriel stood in the doorway of the room, observing the three men whose heads were bowed. Even though these men knew death was not the final end, the loss of a friend still weighed heavy on their hearts.

Gabriel waited for a few moments before entering, because the final chapter in a millennia-long saga was about to unfold. And these men would be at the centre of it all, even though none of them suspected it yet. He closed his eyes and prayed for strength for them.

"Benzahr, Eldad, Lex, my friends," Gabriel said as he entered, touching each of them as he called their names.

They all smiled. It had been a while since they had seen him and they were glad he had come to them now. "Gabriel…" was all Eldad could say in his gruff voice. The other two remained silent. Gabriel looked from man to man and marveled at how different each was to the other.

Benzahr was a sleek banker, with fine extremities, the long limbs and polished features of aristocrats. He came from a long line of old money. His hairline was beginning to recede and thin out at the edges. He was wearing tan-coloured chinos and a grey polo t-shirt tucked in. He looked like he was making a stopover on the way to a golf course. He had a fine Rolex watch on and wore shoes that shone. He always insisted on being called his full name. Only the man that lay dead in the bed now had ever been allowed to call him Zahr. He acknowledged Gabriel with a stiff nod of his head.

Lex was a Mathematics lecturer who doubled as a fitness buff. He was the oldest of the lot, in his early sixties now but looked trimmer and more athletic than Benzahr who was almost twenty years younger. After the loss of his brother, he had turned to fitness as therapy for his sadness. He worked out every day, ate healthy and organic food only and took great care of his body. He liked to wear clothes that showed this off. Today, he was wearing a fitted striped shirt with a pair of blue jeans and loafers. He took and shook Gabriel's hand. His grip was a firm one but his eyes were smiling ones. He had been the closest to the dead man.

Eldad was a short, stocky man with a gruff and loud voice that was well-suited to shouting instructions over the din in his auto-mechanic workshop. He had a love for cars and motorbikes, which bordered on obsessive at times. He was a talker, that one. He said things as they came to his head, without the finesse the other two had.

Different as they were, these men shared a bond that ran deeper and stronger than between blood brothers.

Gabriel ran his hand over Farida's face, shutting his eyes one final time, before picking up the object on his chest. Moments later, they all gathered around a table, all stripped to the waist, except for Gabriel. Each had an intricate tattoo on the left side of the chest, with unique patterns.

Lex asked the question all the others were thinking about. "Gabriel, has the new guardian been selected?"

"The seal always selects its own guardian," Gabriel responded. "For now, we must attend to Farida." He brought the object up to face level. "I have set up a barrier, now it is safe to activate your seals."

He began to recite the words:

>Out of the east

>Out of Eden

>Four flow as one

>One parts into four

>Baruch, Baruch

>Arise and flow

Then each man clasped his hands together.

"Gihon!" Benzahr called.

"Pishon!" Lex exclaimed.

Eldad's "Tigris!" followed.

As each man spoke, streams of light began to appear from the tattoo on his chest. The three lost their earthly clothes and became clad in flaming white armour. Gabriel spoke the name of the last seal, Euphrates. As he did, his garments changed into a fiery white armour that was brighter than that of the other men, and great white wings unfurled on his back. From within his garment, he produced the Keystone and placed it at the centre of the table. Each of the three men proceeded to touch it with both hands. As the final hand touched it, there was a burst of blazing light from the keystone, and then the portal opened. Together, the three carried their companion into Heaven.

Lucan woke up with a start. He could not understand why he had been having the same dream for almost a month. It was not a nightmare. If anything, it left him feeling great. In it, he found himself wrestling a man for what seemed like an eternity. Then the man would touch his leg and his hip would shift, but he would feel no pain. Then the man stretched his hand to give him something but before the thing touched his hand, he would see that the face of the man he had been wrestling with was his own. And then a light would engulf him and he would wake up with a start.

The ringing of his alarm clock brought his thoughts back to the present. Most people used alarms in their Interfacers. But he chose to use an old fashioned alarm clock. It had been a gift from his father when he moved out of the house. Now, it was all he had to remember the man with.

"Today is the day you meet Imani" his Interfacer reminded him.

"Yes!" he exclaimed. His weeks of persistence and patience were finally going to pay off. He got out of bed to prepare for the date. He had one shot at this and he was determined to make it work.

Seven

mani didn't think she would be so nervous when she finally agreed to meet Lucan. But there she was, fiddling with the edge of the tablecloth. Maybe it was because this was her first real date in the true sense of the word. She and her mother had pretty much kept to themselves when she was growing up. Normally, the men would be waiting for her, but she found herself waiting this time.

Lucan straightened his jacket before getting up and walking towards her. He had seen her come in and allowed her to sit down at the table he had reserved. It was a good thing that she knew only his voice. She looked up just as he got to her table. When their eyes met, he knew instantly that she loved him, just as much as he loved her. He had gone through all the phases-realisation, denial and finally submitting himself to his feelings. He was only glad he was behind an Interfacer communication during all of that. If anyone had told him he would be at this point two months before, he would have laughed long and hard. He sat down and smiled, searching for the right words. None came. Suddenly, a call came through on his Interfacer. Darned thing. These people would not leave him be. He let it ring out. But the caller was persistent.

"Excuse me, I have to take this call," he said to Imani. She smiled, saying nothing. He probably had one of the older models, she thought, otherwise he would have known she was the one calling.

"Hello," he said.

"Hello mister," she responded, noticing his widening eyes.

"Why in the world are you calling me when I'm right here?"

"Well, I was beginning to wonder if you talked only through the Interfacer, since you weren't saying anything."

He laughed and ended the call and then looked her in the eye. "Alright, you got me. Now, shall we?"

She smiled in response, relaxing. The magic was not lost.

After an enjoyable evening together, they decided to walk around a park. Imani was glad Lucan had chosen to do the simple things rather than attempt to impress her by taking her to the most expensive or exquisite places. For a girl that grew up on a house in the hills and did not have to contend with the concrete jungle that running her empire required her to live in, the simplicity was a place of escape.

They had not walked for long when a man wearing a peculiar caftan approached them. He had a stiff gait and seemed to belong to a different antique era.

"Greetings, people," he said.

Lucan put himself between the man and Imani. "Good evening sir, how may we help you?"

The man laughed, as if Lucan had said something hysterical. Lucan began to steer himself and Imani away from the man, assuming he was some mad man. But the man followed them, moving surprisingly fast to keep pace.

"Young woman," the man called to Imani. "A great wind is about to blow. It will require you to become that which you fear the most. Before the wind begins to blow, you must seek the Wicket Gate out and pass through it. Thence you will find destiny." Then he paused abruptly and walked away from them.

They turned around immediately and headed back into the restaurant. Lucan helped Imani sit. She had become visibly shaken.

"Let me have a strong drink," Imani said.

Lucan sat with her and held her close, running his hand through her hair.

"It's okay dear, there's nothing to this incident. We won't let it ruin our lovely evening. Let's go home."

She looked up at him, her big eyes captivating him into a sea of desire. She looked so vulnerable now in his arms, nothing like the big media mogul the whole world knew. In that moment, she truly became his woman, to hold and protect. Taking charge now, he helped her up and led her to his own car.

"I'll drop you off at home and ask your chauffeur to take your car home," Lucan said.

Nimrod stood before the cottage in the human body he had chosen. The report he received from the Seers had compelled him to momentarily leave Lucifer's side to investigate for himself. There had been really strong supernatural activity there, definitely. The Seers could only have missed this if there had been an exceptionally strong barrier. He was not sure of the exact source of such barrier, but he would stay on earth to keep an eye on things himself. The last time he had left something Lucifer was personally interested in to be done by subordinates, he had needed all of his wits to escape punishment. Now, he could tell something big was in the offing again. "I must make the best of it this time" he murmured to himself.

Unlike him, Lucifer seemed to be losing a connection to the reality of the things going on, leaving all the direct interaction to his brood of treacherous lieutenants. He, Nimrod, would take charge of things and make sure those vipers didn't get out of hand. He turned and walked to his flying car. "Now, to see to the other matter," he muttered.

"Mum," Imani said, "he looked at me like this..." She was contorting her face in an attempt to replicate the face of the man that accosted her and Lucan during their walk.

Tara threw her head back and laughed. The lines had appeared around her eyes and on her forehead. "The young man, what's his name now..."

"Lucan."

"Yes, Lucan, he must be someone interesting." She rolled her eyes as Imani flushed, and she laughed at the younger woman's embarrassment. "You love him, daughter, and you're falling hard. It's nothing to be ashamed of."

"Oh come off it, mum. You know I don't have the time for…"

Tara's harder laughter interrupted Imani.

Imani stood up and pouted her lips. "Will you even try to take me seriously mum?" Then she joined in laughing too. "I haven't laughed this much for a while, mum. I miss you so much. Why don't you want to join me in town?"

Tara began to answer but Imani interrupted. "I know, I know. You are retired. The city life is just not for you. You'll always be here to refresh me whenever I need it."

Tara became serious. "Now, speaking of matters that are important… Imani, in every madness there is an iota of sanity; in every ranting, an element of truth. When will you make your journey to the Wicket Gate?"

"Mum, you are a scientist, probably the greatest alive," Imani responded. "It is your work that has created the greatest and most revolutionary technology in over a hundred years. But you believe in this Wicket Gate and the life after death in a place called Heaven, which has no scientific basis. You are the greatest paradox, you know?"

Tara sighed. "The most important things in life cannot be proven, cannot be seen and cannot be touched. They must be felt with the heart. Faith, my daughter, faith."

"Maybe someday I will come to believe in this Wicket Gate. But for now, I would rather devote my energies to things that I can see and feel. Have you met anyone who was from or has been to this Heaven? You say you have been to the Wicket Gate, but I ask that you show the way there and you can't. Mum, how do I believe that?" She moved to sit at her mother's feet, placing her head on her laps.

Tara ran her hands through her daughter's hair. "That's coming from the one who had to convince the whole world on the workability of her Direct Buzz Interfacers before they all believed. What drove you even before it was physically real, daughter?"

Imani lifted her head up and her mouth formed to say the words, but then she held herself back.

Tara continued. "You see, when you think about it, we all have faith. What we choose to have faith in is what is important. Some things will not appear to us until we have faith that they are there."

A call came through on Imani's Interfacer. Only few people had this number so it meant the call must be pretty important. She didn't bother to check the caller's Interface ID. She would be able to tell anyone who could get through to her on this line by voice. "Hello," she said as the call connected.

"You better come down here now!" the breathless voice on the other end of the call said. Only one person could talk to her like that. Lulu. Her job description said personal assistant, but she was more of boss than assistant.

"You have been nominated for the Most Influential Tomorrow Leader award!" Lulu continued. "This is super-duper cool! The news has not broken yet; they're keeping it under wraps as they do, but I have my means and I have found out. The award itself is in a week."

"That's huge!" Imani replied with excitement.

"And I'm so sure you will win," Lulu chuckled.

When the call ended, Imani stood up. Her mother followed her movements with her eyes. Imani was enjoying making her mother wait for the gist.

"You better tell me what all that was about, before I spank you silly," Tara said.

Imani laughed. "Oh, mum, you so totally cannot resist a good story. Yours truly has been nominated for the most prestigious young people's award, Most Influential Tomorrow Leader." She took a bow playfully.

Tara played the part of a stunned admirer, clapping and opening her eyes wide. Then she hugged her daughter, and whispered into her ears, "I am so proud of you."

Gabriel sealed the portal and put away the keystone as the four figures emerged. He had chosen not to appear at the cottage this time. There was a small fraction of time between when he came through the portal and when he set up the barrier against any spiritually-aware being that could notice any activity there. The chances were low that such awareness could happen but that night, he had an uneasy feeling. He turned his mind to other matters. The Euphrates seal had chosen its new guardian. He had to be the first to get to him.

Nimrod moved swiftly, not bothering to change from the pyjamas he was wearing. He hadn't come here to be proper for men; his mind was fixed firmly on his goal. Outside, it was blistering cold and the sky was moonless. He cursed having to be confined to this body now. He had to travel the way men travelled and lost time in the process. The Seers that had been monitoring had reported unusual spirit activity that had then disappeared as suddenly as it had appeared. A barrier must have been put up. But the slip up had opened a window of opportunity for him to discover what the source of this activity was. He boarded the waiting flying car. "Fly as fast as the wind here," he said to the driver as he gave him a piece of paper containing the location the Seers had reported.

The dream started as it always did. He was standing outside a tent in nothing but loincloth. His opponent appeared and they began to wrestle and finally he touched and shifted his hip. For the first time in the dreams, the man spoke to him.

"What do men call you?" he asked.

"I am Lucan," he responded.

"You are Euphrates." The man said in a booming voice.

Suddenly he was standing beside a river bank. When he looked into the water, his reflection was as clear as though he was looking into a mirror. But this was no mere mirror effect. His reflection was wearing a white, shining chain mail armour and was carrying a huge flaming sword. It seemed to have a light of its own flowing out of it. Captivated by this, he looked on and marvelled. Suddenly, the reflection rose out of the water and held him. He had wanted to flee, but his body refused to react. It looked him in the eye and said, "Euphrates."

That was when he woke up. The warm feeling was missing this time. He yearned for the light. He sat up, pondering what it all meant. Suddenly, he felt it - the feeling he was yearning. It was even crazy that he could remember a feeling from a dream and feel it in reality. But he wasn't in any doubt that it was the same feeling. His eyes darted around furtively in the darkness, half expecting to see the man he wrestled in the dream. His eyes fell on the pillow beside him. On it, was an object about the size of his finger, glowing softly. Something told him this was what he had not been able to touch in the dreams. He reached for it hesitantly and picked it up. As his hands touched it, a surge of energy went through him like nothing he had ever experienced before and his whole vision exploded into light. For a period of time he could not determine, he could see nothing but the light.

When the light cleared, he was on the floor lying on his back. As his vision adjusted to the darkness of his room, he realised he was not alone. Someone was kneeling beside him. He tried to get up, but strong arms held him down.

"You will get up and come with me if you want to understand what is happening to you," the man said.

A question began to form on his lips, but it was as if the man could read his thoughts, and so the man cut him off.

"No question you ask can be answered here," the man said earnestly, "you must come with me now, Lucan. There are those who seek you and must not find you."

Much as he disliked being told what to do, Lucan sensed that he needed to go with this fellow. "You will at least allow me to change into more appropriate clothes," he tried.

"Please go ahead, but do it quickly," the man said as he eased the pressure that had held Lucan's arms down. Lucan got up and switched on the lights in the room, seeing the man who had held him down for the first time.

"I am Gabriel," the man declared. "Now quit looking at me and get dressed!"

"I need to know where you are taking me. What is happening to me? Why am I wrestling myself in my dreams? Why have I been dreaming the same dream for one month? I need answers, or I am not moving an inch."

Humans and their endless questions. They did not know to obey and freewill constrained him from moving Lucan. He sighed.

"Lucan, we need to make haste. Do you have a bible anywhere here?" Gabriel asked.

Lucan pointed to a thick, antique bible on his shelf. The book always fascinated him and when a book fascinated him, he made sure he got a physical copy for keeps.

"Pick it up, Lucan. The answers you seek start from in there. I hope you know how to find things in it," he said

Lucan nodded.

"Good, on the ride, you'll read the twenty eight' chapter of Genesis, from verse ten to twenty two. Then go to Genesis chapter two and read verses ten to fourteen. Finally, read chapter thirty three from verse twenty two to thirty one," Gabriel instructed.

"I've read that book a few times. What will I find in it that I have not seen already?" Lucan responded.

"Lucan," Gabriel called, "every moment you spend here puts you in very real danger. Sometimes, it is in your obedience that you will find answers to your questions." The urgency in Gabriel's voice spurred Lucan to make haste. He undressed quickly. In the process, he looked at himself on the full length mirror out of habit. What he saw startled him. On his left chest, an intricate tattoo that had not been there before was now a prominent feature. He quickly put on a sweatshirt and a pair of jeans.

Nimrod was back in his apartment. Day was just breaking and he had ordered coffee and toast. From the description of the Seers, it had to be a very powerful angel that was responsible for this. What he could not decide was whether this manifestation was an answer to a man's freewill prayer or a sovereign action. Powerful angels sometimes intervened on behalf of men in answer to prayers. But if this was indeed a sovereign action, then something big was up. He would keep this from Lucifer. The Seers had been warned on the pain of Tartarus to report to Nimrod alone. No other demon lieutenant must know of this except him. All of them had taken human form in preparation for The Bringing. They were all attending because Lucifer himself was coming. Nimrod hooked up the Interfacers and placed a conference call to the other lieutenants. He liked these Interfacer things; they were sort of like spirit communication. "Lilith, you will make the announcement of the nominees tomorrow. I'm sure you can handle that".

"Do not order me around, worm!" Lilith growled.

"Okay, do not do it then, we will just appoint someone else to do the honours," Nimrod retorted.

"Lilith, we all know you want to do this, so just cut the chase and go get it done," Abadon said when he cut in. "I was in the middle of interesting things here with these human women. I really do not want this to drag. Goodbye." With that, he ended his own connection.

"You'll have yours come to you one of these days, Nimrod darling," Lilith said with niceness that dripped venom before she ended the call.

Lucan had had the presence of mind to put a call through to Imani as he followed Gabriel from his apartment in the wee hours of the morning. Her nomination would be announced that day and he would have loved to celebrate that with her. But the events of the few hours before had put paid to all other plans. He needed to understand what was happening to him. He thumbed through the portions Gabriel had asked him to read. He exclaimed suddenly. "This is my dream. This is exactly what happens in my dream. The only detail missing is the man trying to give something to me and the light engulfing me."

"That detail was left out. Deliberately. Because of the power in what you received today. Jacob was the first Guardian of the Seals."

"I don't understand. What seals?" Lucan responded.

"In Eden of the East, there were four rivers. Each seal is one of the rivers. Did you see the stone Jacob placed his head on when he saw the ladder of angels?"

Lucan nodded.

"That is the keystone. The seals are the keys and the keystone is the door."

"To?" Lucan asked

"Where the angels coming up and down the ladder come from. Heaven." Gabriel responded.

"So you mean there are three other people like me?"

"Precisely. And we are going to meet them here," Gabriel responded.

Lucan looked up from the book. They had come to a portion of the city that he had never really gone to before. It was where the city's super-rich lived. He wondered why Imani did not live there, even though she could very well afford it. Now that he was passing through its streets, he could guess why. The houses had a forbidding look to them, as if they were silently telling you that you were unwelcome there. There was a stuffy, uptight feeling in the air. High fences and huge gates effectively hid most of the interior of the houses away from the view of passers-by. He had observed that they had not met anyone on the roads as they drove in. Life here was secluded, isolated and rigid. They would probably look down on people like Imani as nouveau riche.

They got to a gate that was huge even by the general standards of this section, with a seal of Solomon carved in its centre. As they approached the gate, it rolled open to allow them in and slowly shut behind them once they entered. They drove for another three minutes along a winding driveway before reaching the main house. Then they bypassed the main house and went all the way around to a patio in the back. There, three men were already seated on palm-shaped seats. It was minutes past seven, but the day was just beginning to become bright. When he got close enough to make out the faces, he could recognise one. Seated in the middle of the group, slender and brooding, was the rich banker Benzahr Phocas. He was old, old money.

They all stood to greet Gabriel before taking their seats again. Gabriel signaled for Lucan to take a seat beside him. Then he placed his hand on Lucan's shoulder and announced, "the Euphrates seal's choice, Lucan Belgore."

The well-built middle-aged man leaned forward and made introductions. "I am Lex Cole, and this is Eldad Beriah. You probably know Benzahr already, you see him all the time on your Interfacer news. You are probably wondering what is happening to you. All of us seated here, at least except Gabriel, have gone through that." He turned to the rest of the men and nodded. The three men stood up and stripped to their waists. Lucan stared wide-eyed as he saw tattoos as intricate as his own on each man's left chest. "Wow" he exclaimed.

"Yes Lucan, you are not alone." Eldad said in his gruff voice.

"All is ready," Gabriel interjected. Then he swung his hands in the air and commanded, "Lift up your heads, O ye gates, and be ye lifted, ye everlasting doors!"

At that, there was a rumbling, and the stone floor of the patio parted into two, revealing a stairway going down into the ground. One by one, the men stepped onto the top of the stairway and disappeared into the brightness below. When it was just the two of them left standing on the edge, Gabriel turned to Lucan and said, "Your turn, Lucan." Lucan looked at him, unsure if he should proceed. Gabriel nodded reassuringly. "I'll be right behind you, but you need to go now."

He braced himself up and took the first step into the opening. Almost immediately his feet touched the first step, he was standing alone. The step he stood on seemed to detach itself from the stairway and float upwards, rather than downwards as he had expected. When he burst through the light, the three men were standing on the banks of a river. The landscape reminded him of somewhere he had seen and been before, but he couldn't place his finger on it. Everything here seemed to be in high definition. The green of the grass was greener, the water sparkling clearer than any he had ever seen. The sun here was bright and warm, but not scorching. Even the air he was breathing felt different. Every breath seemed to draw invigoration into his bones. He could feel it coursing through him.

When he turned, Gabriel was standing by his side. "This, my friend is The Secret Place. I presume you were here earlier today. Here, we can safely show you who you have become."

"I'll go first," Eldad said. Lucan watched as Eldad placed his hand on his chest and hollered "Tigris!" Instantly, Eldad became covered in light. It lasted for a few moments, lifting him off his feet a few feet above the ground. When it cleared, he was clad in armour like the reflection Lucan had seen in the water in the dream. That jolted his memory. This was the river bank he had seen in his dream, but he never thought it was a real place. As he watched on, the other two men did the same, calling out a different name each time and were transformed. Then Gabriel too morphed before his eyes into an angel, with the huge wings, white gleaming robe and fiery sword old paintings showed angels carrying.

Lucan just stood there, believing he would wake up again soon in his own bed. He heard Gabriel's voice, more with his being than ears.

"Name your seal, Lucan," he commanded.

"But what is its name?" Lucan responded.

"You know it already. You only need to listen hard enough."

"To who? To what?"

"To yourself, Lucan. To yourself alone. Now listen."

Lucan closed his eyes and with supreme effort began to clear his mind of all the spectacular events that was going on around him. Moments of quietness passed before he remembered his reflection's whisper, and his lips formed the word "Euphrates." The surge that raced through his body nearly knocked him off his feet. He opened his eyes as he struggled to keep his footing. When he finally steadied himself, he saw that light was beginning to emanate from his left chest, and from there it covered his whole being. When it all cleared, he had become exactly as his reflection had been in his dream.

Gabriel placed a hand on his shoulder and said, "Now we can begin."

To Lucan, it seemed they had been in The Secret Place for years, but in reality, they had been there for just one day. Eldad had explained to him with a slap on his back that a day was as a thousand years and a thousand years as a day in that realm. Confusing, but Lucan did not bother to query further. While there, he had been taken through time to the origin of the seal, and he had seen the millennia of man on earth. He had witnessed the fall and the invasion of the angels and the flood. He had watched Jacob wrestle and receive the seal and seen how through the years, many had sought the seal. And he had seen the one behind the many schemes, Lucifer, and his fallen demons. With this power, he would be able to see and hear them even while they were in human forms. He would be able to banish them to Tartarus. But with the power came great responsibility. He felt he could handle all of them except one. All the others required that he restrained his head, but one required that he stopped listening to his heart. He said nothing of this to the other guardians or Gabriel, the holder of the keystone. He stayed on with them until they all left for their homes. It was only when he got to the crowded part of town that he began to understand how his life would be radically different. He would never have believed anything of what he now saw.

All around, there were demons in human form. He walked past some having a snack and chatting with other normal humans. He could hear the demons constantly communicating with one another in what Gabriel had told him was spirit communication. A whole new world had opened up to his senses. The supernatural had been around him all along but he just couldn't see it. Now it lay plain before him. He hurried along to the privacy of his house.

Imani couldn't believe how happy she was to hear his voice when Lucan's call came in that evening. She had really missed him and she didn't even bother to try to hide it. She was glad when it was clear that he had equally missed her. "My mother has been dying to meet you," Imani said. "I'm planning to take the whole of tomorrow off. We are going to see her."

"You didn't add, 'And that's an order!'" Lucan chuckled.

She laughed too. "Love you."

"Love you too, babe," he purred back and ended the call.

When Tara's doorbell rang, she wondered who it could be at that time of evening. Imani was not due to appear with her boyfriend till the next morning. She put down the book she was reading and adjusted her reading glasses. She then slipped into the fuzzy slippers Imani had got her and padded to the door lazily. She didn't notice it was opened until she stretched her hand to open it. Panic flooded through her and she turned to run into the house. As she swung around, strong arms caught her. She was about to scream for help when she looked up into familiar brown eyes. "Gabriel!" she shouted. "I haven't seen you since…" she paused to catch her breath. "You gave me such a scare; you haven't changed at all."

Gabriel laughed. "You still always try to say more than one thing at a time when you see me, Tara. That has not changed." He held her a little distance from himself and gave a look over her. "The years have been kind to you."

She laughed and led him into the living area of the house.

"You totally forgot us," Tara said as they settled in a seat. "Not even once did you stop by in all these years."

Gabriel shifted in his chair into a more comfortable position. "I go only where I am sent; not my will, but His. I would have loved more than nothing else to come, but I wasn't sent here till now."

Tara sighed. She knew he spoke the truth. He was an angel after all and there were many important supernatural events he had to attend to than to be interested in the whims of a mortal woman who didn't see other mortal men like herself to love.

"And how is the little girl?" he ventured.

"Imani?"

"Do you have any other?"

Tara laughed. "Are we going to have a conversation entirely made up of questions? As you say, questions always lead to more questions."

Gabriel recalled that was the first thing he said to her and they both laughed. When they stopped, he went back to his question. "How is she?"

"She is not so little anymore, for starters. She's a big woman now."

Tara was avoiding the question even though it was clear to him she knew what he was really asking. "Does she believe yet?" Gabriel pressed.

Tara noticed his face had done those playful to serious shifts. She sighed, sinking deeper into her chair. "No she doesn't. I wish I could believe for her, wish I could do this for her, but you know better than I do that she must find this belief herself for the path to the Wicket Gate to even appear to her."

Gabriel paced for a bit before he spoke again. "Tara, the world is at a precipice. Good and evil are about to clash one final time. She will be the deciding factor on the fate of this world."

"Gabriel, she is my world. The whole world would not mean a thing to me if…"

"Tara!" Gabriel scolded. "You cannot allow your love for her to cloud your understanding of her destiny."

Tara broke into tears at his rebuke.

Gabriel walked over to her and put his arm around her. When he spoke, his voice was tenderer. "I didn't mean to bring you to tears, dear one. I really do understand how you feel. But she will not be safe until she believes. We must believe in her then. It's all we can do now."

Then he was gone. Tara sat alone. This was why she knew it was futile to feel anything for an angel. He would always leave when he was commanded to and would never be able to return her love, and she would be alone again. But those months with him during her pregnancy and after Imani's birth had been so magical that she had never been able to bring herself to love any other man. It just seemed like she was settling for something less with all other men. She sighed deeply. "I'm just a stupid dreamy old woman," she said to herself ruefully. She breathed a prayer through her tears for her daughter.

Lucan realised his nervousness had been unfounded after his first five minutes with Imani's mum that morning. She had been warm and easy to get along with and seemed to like him. And he had seen a new Imani today. Being with her mum brought out the playful child in her and he was really glad to see her that way. She was trying out dresses she wanted to wear for the award event for them.

"This one makes you look like a peacock in display," her mum teased. Imani made faces at her before going back in to change the dress. While she was gone, Tara turned to Lucan and asked suddenly, "What do you think of the Wicket Gate?"

Lucan hesitated. He had been able to deduce that Imani didn't believe in the Wicket Gate and was unsure if she got that disbelief from her mother or otherwise. He would tread carefully. "It only appears to those who believe it is," he responded, hand on chin.

Tara leaned forward and looked him in the eye. "Do you believe, Lucan?"

Lucan held her gaze and said in almost a whisper, "I believe." Tara kept her eyes on him for a few more seconds, as if probing his sincerity, and then, satisfied, she sat back into the chair.

Imani came out in a fitted silver dress, flowing like a goddess. "Mum, could you help me with the zipper, please," she asked, turning her back to her mum.

Tara gave Lucan a knowing look and said with meaning, "Help her."

EiGHt

ucan fidgeted with his tie while he waited for Imani to get ready. The days had flown by and before they knew it, the day of the award ceremony had come. All over the media, the buzz had been high. Regular Interfacer broadcasts had kept coming and voting had reached a fevered pitch towards the closing hours of the polls. Now, the moment they had been waiting for was here.

The sound of the door opening brought Lucan out of his thoughts and he looked in that direction. Standing in the doorway, looking like someone who had stepped out of a beautiful painting, was the woman he loved. All other thoughts flew out of his mind in that instant. He was transfixed by the vision of her beauty. She took each step with grace and elegance, seeming to float through the air towards him. He was not aware that his mouth had opened until she reached him and laughingly closed it.

"Was it worth the wait?" she asked.

"Oh, I'd wait a thousand years, if necessary, to behold thy fair form, thou fairest of all." He was laughing and bowing.

"Lucan, I'm nervous," Imani said with seriousness.

He held her hands with one hand and put the other around her shoulder. "Don't be dear. I'll be by your side every step today, ok?" He planted a kiss on her cheek and then whispered into her ear in the same breath, "You'll be wonderful."

Nimrod sat behind a huge mahogany desk as he ran through his checklist one more time. The result of the voting had been given to the announcer. He had done one final check to make sure the name in the envelope was the correct one. He could not afford to let anything go wrong on this night. The award show had to be the greatest the world had ever seen. Three multiple award-winning musicians had been contracted to perform. The hall being used had been decorated from the scratch to resemble an Olympian event. Nimrod clasped his hands together and muttered a phrase. Instantly, the wall behind him disappeared, revealing a huge room. The room was dark, with dim light supplied by actual torches arranged sparsely along the walls on both sides. The central item in the room was a huge marble altar that had marble seats arranged around it.

The Seers were walking around the altar, burning incense and chanting in their hissing voices. Nimrod couldn't interrupt their chanting, so he spoke with spirit communication.

"Is all set for the master?" he asked.

"All is set, master," the leader of the Seers replied. Nimrod knew Lucifer liked order and what represented order today was that Lucifer expected the sacrifice to be performed on the stroke of midnight of this February 29, a day that occurred once every leap year. Nimrod was not usually a nervous one, but he found himself shaky that day. It must be the human form he was in, he reasoned. He couldn't wait for this to be over.

Imani was grateful to have Lucan with her for the award event. She was a serious corporate mogul and not an entertainment personality. The paparazzi were unbearable. But as an award-winning author, Lucan was used to them and he skillfully guided her through their madness. Imani's assistant, Lulu, handled the paparazzi once Lucan had guided Imani past them to the red carpet. He stayed by her side all through the red carpet moments and helped her maintain her smile and poise. "You're doing great dear," he kept saying with a huge smile.

The hall was amazing. Imani fitted perfectly into the Olympian setting with her Greek gown. After the headlining performance of the night, it was time for the grand finale. Imani crossed her fingers and waited for the announcers to name the winner.

Even though he was doing everything to keep Imani calm through the event, Lucan himself was anything but calm. This was a den of demons, he knew it. Their presence made his skin crawl. All around, he could see their hideous forms camouflaged in human skin. He felt something ominous about this gathering. There was something going on here. He made up his mind that he would not let Imani out of his sight that night. And once the award was over, he would get her out of there as fast as he could. The announcer was about to announce the winner. He hoped it wouldn't be Imani. He didn't need this night to be any longer than necessary. They needed to get out of there. Fast.

"And the winner is…" The announcer paused for effect. A hush went over the whole arena. "Imani!"

It took Imani moments to realise that she was the one called. Again, Lucan came to her rescue, helping her to her feet and ushering her to the stage. By the time she got to the stage, she had composed herself. She went through her acceptance speech smoothly. As she got off the stage, her arm in Lucan's, a flurry of photographers' flashes went off. The images would be on every news medium in a matter of moments.

Imani and Lucan were ushered away from the hall into an exclusive office with a huge mahogany desk as its centrepiece. There was a huge monitor on the wall, where a live streaming of the award was ongoing. One of the artistes was giving the final performance of the night. A middle-aged, bespectacled man sat behind the desk. Seated on either side of the man were three other men of varying ages and one very beautiful woman. They all wore dark suits, except the woman, who wore a short gown. They exuded power.

"Congratulations, Imani," the man behind the desk said in a rich voice.

Lucan was alarmed. No, alarmed was an understatement. They had just been ushered into a room full of the most powerful demons he had ever seen in his short career as a guardian. It was clear to him now that the whole award had been set up by these demons. Why they had set this up was unclear to him. But whatever the reason, he knew it wasn't just to give back to the world or fuzzy things like that. He tuned in to see if they were saying anything in the spirit. Silence. What should he do?

"And this is my fiancé, Lucan Belgore," Imani was saying.

"The same Belgore, the bestselling author?" asked the woman.

Lucan looked at her and saw her true form- a huge serpentine being. He nearly fell out of his chair. He made an attempt to compose himself. "Pleasure to meet you ma'am."

Then the demons began to talk in the spirit. What Lucan heard was his greatest fear. They wanted to separate him from Imani.

The man behind the desk spoke to Imani. "We need to discuss some confidential business matters with you. Mr. Belgore will have to excuse us."

Imani turned to Lucan. He was trying to tell her something but she just couldn't get it. Why couldn't he just say it? She gave him a probing look, and he held her gaze. Something about the way he looked at her made her decide that she preferred to have him with her for the discussion. She turned to the man. "Lucan will be staying with us through all the discussions we will have sir."

"I beg your pardon," one of the other men who hadn't spoken since they got in responded.

"These discussions are very high level and confidential," the woman cut in. "We simply cannot have him there."

When Imani turned to Lucan again, his heart sank to the ground. He knew she was about to ask him to allow them discuss the business privately. The door opened and a huge man came in to usher him to an adjoining room. Another demon. Lucan quickly asked, "How long is this going to take sir?" He directed his question at the man behind the desk, looking at him frankly for the first time. He was a thin, big-headed demon, but he seemed to be the most powerful of the pack.

The man looked at the clock on the wall. It was eleven thirty. "It will take only thirty minutes at most," he replied stiffly. Then he turned to the aide. "Take care of Mr. Belgore while he waits."

Lucan sat on the edge of his seat in the brightly lit room. There were two aides in the room with him, and it seemed as though they were keeping him under watch rather than attending to him. Fifteen minutes had passed and there had been no word from the adjoining room. He kept looking at the wall clock until it seemed the time was not moving fast enough. He decided to listen in on the aides to see if they were engaged in any spirit communication. All he could hear them repeating was "The Bringing." It appeared that that was what the night was about, this Bringing. He wondered how Imani was linked to all this. He had never heard of any Bringing before and Gabriel had certainly not told him anything about it. He kept listening to them.

"I wish I could be at the sacrifice tonight," the aide closer to Lucan communicated to his partner. "Lord Lucifer himself is making an appearance."

Lucan was destabilised. Sacrifice? Lucifer? Who was the…

The aide continued talking in the spirit, interrupting Lucan's thoughts. "But when the sacrifice brings trash along, I have to dispose of the trash and miss out on the fun."

What! Imani was the sacrifice and what they were bringing was Lucifer. Lucan kicked himself for letting her out of his sight. What kind of man was he to leave his woman in the hands of demons in the name of being civil? Without warning, he shot out of his seat and took the one closer to him out with one hit to the windpipe. The other one was too startled by his sudden movement to make a move. By the time he pulled out his gun, Lucan was upon him. There was a brief scuffle and Lucan forced him to drop the gun. He was about to call for backup when Lucan hit him in the kidneys. Seconds later, the scuffle was over.

Lucan stole a glance at the wall clock. Eleven fifty-five. He needed to find Imani before the thirty minutes was over. He went over the aide's body that lay crumpled on the floor and raced into the room where Imani was with the demons. What he saw shocked him. The wall behind the big desk was totally gone. In the spot it had been, he saw a huge room further in.

"What the hell?" he exclaimed. Quickly, he scaled the desk into the room. He didn't know how close to hell he really was.

If the absence of the wall startled him, what he saw in the room nearly sent him reeling backwards. Imani was laid out on a large marble altar in the centre of the room, bound and gagged. Huge, hooded demons were burning incense and chanting as they circled the altar. The five that had met him and Imani earlier surrounded the altar and the one that had been behind the desk stood at Imani's head, a curved, sharp marble knife in his hands.

"An extra dead body would hurt no one," the man said in the spirit. Out of the shadows, demons began to close in on Lucan. They were not in human form. They had released their eni forms, so humans must have invoked them. Then, Lucan noticed the bodies on the ground. These demons had slain their invokers. He looked at Imani and their eyes met. All he saw was raw fear in her eyes. The struggle in his mind was only fleeting. He had no choice in this. "Sorry guys," he muttered as he closed his eyes. Then he hit his left chest and breathed, "Euphrates."

Light engulfed his body and in an instant, he was transformed. The light he emitted illuminated the room and the once dark room became as bright as the noonday. All around, the dark forms of demons huddled together to avoid his light. The five demon lords could have been stone where they stood. They looked in utter amazement. He swung his sword in one direction and white light shot in an arc in that direction. All the demons that fell under its light were consumed by it in an instant. Their screaming as they descended into Tartarus was blood curdling. Lucan ignored this as he sent white flames in every direction of the room. Over the screams of the banished demons, he heard the leader of the five calling for their own invokers. Lucan knew he needed to end the battle before they were invoked. He sensed he would be unable to handle the five demon lords simultaneously if they released their eni forms. And if they were high ranking enough, they might have eji forms when their full power would be unleashed. He closed his eyes and issued the command, "Occupy, Euphrates."

As soon as he did, the room began to fill up with flowing, liquid light. The demons struggled to escape it. Faster than any of them could react, the room had filled up to the brim. Lucan stood guard at the entrance, cutting down every demon that got away from the light-filled room. Not a single one escaped; he made sure of that. When the liquid light receded, only the bodies of the five demon lords and a wide-eyed Imani remained in the room. He approached the altar and removed her gag.

"Don't touch me!" she screamed once her gag was off, trembling. "Who are you? What are you? What were they?"

"It's okay dear, I'm the good guy," Lucan said, trying to go near her again.

"Lucan Belgore, you will stay where you are and explain yourself before taking any further step towards me." Being as shaken as she was didn't stop her from being stubborn.

"We are not safe here yet. Let's get you out of here first." He picked her up as if she was a feather and opened a portal. In the twinkling of an eye, they were in his room at home. Using the portal after using the occupy command had left him weakened. Quickly, he returned to his normal state and tried to joke. "Like me better this way?"

Imani did not even bat an eyelid. She was still visibly flustered, but calmer. "You'd better start explaining what just happened or I will leave here this moment."

Lucan sighed and looked into her eyes. "I am a Guardian of the Seal," he began.

Gabriel did not understand the instruction. From the day Adam and Even had been ejected from the garden, he had been the keeper of the keystone. But today, he had been commanded to leave it in the mansion. They knew a lot - angels, but even an archangel like him did not know the full plan and purpose. That was why they had to obey the only One who did.

Gabriel sensed the release of a seal and the release of demons in the distance. He lifted up his eyes.

"It has finally begun," he said.

Nimrod was filled with wrath as he descended into Neatherworld, his wiry form twisting from side to side, his eyes the colour of glowing embers. He had had the presence of mind to kill his human body with the marble knife before that cursed river of light hit him in the room. That suicide had been his saving grace, releasing him from the body the instant it died. Otherwise, he would have been languishing in Tartarus now, like those other fools, who could not think on their feet.

How could he not have sensed it? How could he not have known? A Guardian of the Seal had walked into their midst and they hadn't recognised him. He had prided himself in his sense of perception; it was what he felt set him apart from the rest. Yet, the ultimate prize had been within his grasp and they had been focusing on some silly distraction of a sacrifice. On top of that, he had to explain to Lucifer how The Bringing had failed on his watch and how he was the only survivor. Now he knew how those demons he had saved many times from Lucifer's wrath have felt when approaching the throne after a failure. But he was a survivor. He would not escape Tartarus on earth just to come to Neatherworld and still be banished there.

Imani would never have believed a word that Lucan had told her before now. But after what she had seen, she knew he was telling her the truth. He was a Guardian of the Seal, a line that ran all the way from Jacob, the Israelite patriarch, to him. There were others and they had those powers she had seen him display, and more. He was stripped to the waist now and she could see the tattoos on his chest just as he had said. That was only one piece of the puzzle. Just as surprising was the discovery she had also made that evening- not every human being around was really human. There were demons - supernatural evil beings, disguised as humans in their midst. She had seen some of them battle Lucan. They had nearly killed her in some bizarre ritual. And he had talked about the Wicket Gate. With all this, she had to believe that the Wicket Gate was indeed real. She was still unsure of many things though, especially when it came to her relationship with Lucan.

"Lucan, will this change things between us?" she asked.

"I don't want it to. It doesn't have to. Being a guardian won't have any meaning if you were not in my life or if it was the reason I lost you." He was holding her in his arms.

"Lucan, nothing can change my love for you, absolutely nothing. I love you so much… more than life."

Lucan heaved a sigh of relief.

"I will stay with you till the day breaks," she continued. "I'll be going to my mother's in the morning to clear my head. I need to be sure I can handle the responsibility of being your woman, knowing everything I know now."

Lucan panicked. "What are you saying? Because of what you know now, you want to leave me? But you said you…"

"Hush, Lucan," Imani cut in, placing one finger on his lips. "I cannot not be your woman. It's not a possibility. But I need time to brace myself up for it. And I need to see my mother about the Wicket Gate. She's been there before. She will be able to guide me."

"Alright dear," Lucan responded. He didn't want her out of his sight for one moment, but he knew she was making sense. "I'll go there with you tomorrow."

"That's fine."

Within minutes of lying down, Imani was asleep.

"There is a traitor in our midst, my Lord," Nimrod said emphatically as he finished reporting the events of the night to Lucifer. He stood aside, watching and waiting. Lucifer seemed to brood for a couple of moments. Those moments were torturous for Nimrod. Then Lucifer stood from his throne. "Nimrod," he said when he began. "You are my top lieutenant. I know of your rivalry with the other lieutenants. How am I to know that you are not the traitor that revealed the secrets of The Bringing in order to eliminate them? It would not be beyond a fiend like you to try something like that. I could if I was in your shoes."

Any other demon would try to speak in defense at this moment, but Nimrod's experience made him hold back.

Lucifer continued. "But even then, the enemy would never act in that rash manner except the girl was so important that they had to. Have you investigated this?"

"I rushed here to report this to you first my lord," Nimrod answered. "I will do that right away." He saw some expression he could not read on Lucifer's face as he returned to his throne.

From beside Lucifer's throne, a huge housefly-shaped demon emerged. "Beelzebub will go with you to the earth on this task, seeing now that you have no one else to help you," Lucifer said. "I have invokers waiting ready for you, so you will not be restricted by human bodies on this task. I sense that it is important enough to take those risks."

Nimrod felt an anger rise from deep within his twisted body. What this meant was that he was being watched by Lucifer. His master was not as rusty as he had thought. He had withheld one small bit of information in his report to Lucifer- the identity of the one who had attacked the Bringing. And Lucifer had not asked.

Lucan dropped Imani off at her mother's early the next morning. He hadn't slept for even a second throughout the night. He had pondered on the first thing he would say to her when she woke up, something that would ensure the day did not start off with any stiffness. But he had been unable to come up with anything. He hadn't needed it though. Her words when she did wake up were, "Hey darling, what's for breakfast?"

That had broken any ice that he thought had formed. He made some toast and coffee before he took her home. He had done all he could to hide his worries during the journey to Tara's place. He watched Imani go right up to the door before turning the vehicle away. He needed to find Gabriel.

Nimrod watched from the shadows as the flying car made its way into the air. He was glad now that a junior demon like Beelzebub was all Lucifer had left to attach to him. Those ones were so used to taking orders that when he had directed Beelzebub to go to the site of The Bringing to investigate the spiritual substance of the attackers, the fool had made no objections to the idea. Now that Nimrod was sure that Beelzebub's attention had shifted elsewhere, he was alone to continue with his plan. He would wait for five minutes to make sure the Guardian was gone before making any move into the house.

Although the visit was unexpected, Tara embraced her daughter without asking questions. This was her home, and her daughter was welcome anytime.

They had hardly sat down before the words tumbled out of Imani. "Tell me all about the Wicket Gate, mum."

That request knocked Tara's wind out. She was tempted to ask what had happened, but she decided to answer her daughter's questions rather than ask her own. "At the very beginning of our world, man was created immortal, exactly like God. But we were deceived to think we needed to become like Him, when we already were in His image. In the quest to become what we already were, we lost what we were. Our immortality and connection to the Creator were lost and ultimately death was introduced." She paused and saw the get-to-the-point look in Imani's eyes. "The Wicket Gate is the hope of all men. It is a gate within a gate, shrouded in the Presence. The path to it is long for some and short for others. It is unique to each individual. Your path will appear to you only when you fully believe and out of your own freewill, you confess this belief with both your lips and your heart. Do you truly believe, my daughter?"

Imani's lips were forming the words to answer when she saw it. She froze midsentence. Her eyes widened with fear and her hands began trembling where she placed them on her knees. Her mother followed her gaze and the hairs on the back of her neck stood at what she saw. Coming towards them was a monstrous creature. It seemed to ooze evil out of its being. It had a huge eye and a horn prominent on its face. It filled the room with pungent yellow smoke that made them choke.

Tara opened her mouth to scream but no sound came out. She heard Imani muttering repeatedly, "Not again, not again..." as though she had seen it before. The creature was moving in Imani's direction speedily. Tara jumped up and stood between the creature and her daughter, willing herself to stay alert in the haze. Just its presence had transformed her living room into a little hell.

As the creature got close, she looked into eyes that burnt with a consuming hatred. Its gaze overwhelmed her and she fell to her knees. She tried to speak again, but her voice failed her one more time. Visions of Lamela on that fateful day and ritual ceremonies in which similar creatures were invoked while she was at The Place flooded her memory. The bloodlust of these creatures was clear in her mind. The creature had risen to the ceiling, looking down at them. Then, without warning, it dived down at lightening speed and picked her daughter. She tried to touch the creature, but her hand simply slipped through it as if she was trying to grasp smoke. Without taking notice of her efforts, it rose up and hovered in the ceiling again.

It began to speak to her. She heard it not with her ears, but with her being, similar to the way she heard Gabriel. "Tell Lucan he must come to the Plain of New Megiddo with all the seals by midnight today, or the girl dies," it said. "I trust that you will tell him very convincingly."

Without another word, it opened a dark hole in the ceiling and went through it with Imani, leaving behind the hazy smoke to remind Tara that this was no dream. She screamed with the anguish of a mother who was watching her child being led to an inevitable death.

The four guardians were gathered in Benzahr's mansion, where Lucan had first been introduced to the rest of the guardians. Lucan had called for this meeting after receiving Tara's message. He had rushed to Tara's to see her, but she just sat there, wordlessly looking at him with a void expression in her eyes. It moved him to tears. The last time he had seen her, she had been a lively and somewhat mischievous woman. He had seen a husk sucked dry of her essence today. He was going to save Imani. There were two of them who couldn't live without her.

At the moment, he was making a passionate appeal to the rest of the guardians to help him get her back.

"You need to help me get her back," he pleaded. "Her mother blames me for her abduction because the demon specifically mentioned my name. I love this woman and cannot lose her, dear friends."

Eldad rose up, pounding his fist on the table. "Do not spew such nonsense, you impulsive brat. You expect us to jeopardize the whole earth by revealing ourselves for the safety of this one woman?"

"Calm down Eldad," Benzahr moderated.

"How can I? To think that he would use his powers so rashly so soon… it's just irresponsible." Eldad kept on banging his thick fist on the table.

Lucan stood up too, eyes flashing. "I did what I had to do! Was I supposed to just sit there and allow her to be killed?"

Eldad and Lucan threw daggers across the table with their eyes.

Benzahr got up and placed a hand on each man's shoulder. He spoke calmly. "Sit down, both of you." It was a request but it sounded more like an order. They both obeyed the older guardian. Then he turned to Lex. "You might want to tell the rookie your story."

Lex looked squarely at Lucan as he began his story. "Every great responsibility will require great sacrifice. Each of us around this table has had to make tough choices because we are guardians. It comes with the terrain. I grew up with only one brother, he was ten years younger than me, and I loved him like a son. We were orphaned early and I had to grow up fast to take care of him. A few years after I became a guardian, he got into the university where I lecture. You see, love can blind even the most rational of us, as it is about to do to you now. Things got out of hand when my brother joined a biker group who were actually the local coven of invokers on campus. I did all that was possible to convince him to rethink that decision but such things have a way of gripping the heart with a conviction that is difficult to shake. I watched my brother die when the demons did what they have done to Imani to him. They held him and dared me to use my power. I had to choose between his life and the destruction of the world."

"So you folded your hands and did nothing as they killed your own brother for the seal? Even though you could save him?" Lucan asked with his eyes burning with anger.

Lex looked at him pointedly. "I did what I knew was the right thing to do!"

"Then I will do what my heart tells me is right now, with or without your help," Lucan shouted, jumping to his feet again.

Eldad jumped up. "Can't you see that you'll be walking into a trap? Or do you think they will be surprised again like the first time you encountered them? No, damn it, they'll be ready this time. They've picked the place and time. Think, rookie, think!"

"I will rather die trying than live knowing there was a chance to save her life that I didn't take," Lucan responded. "Of what use is saving the world if I cannot save my world?"

For a brief moment, one could hear a pin drop there. Then Benzahr spoke what they had all been thinking. "You forget as a guardian that death is not the end. Even if she dies, you can always go into Heaven to see her, isn't it? So listen to the voice of reason." He placed a hand on Lucan's shoulder. "Let it go Lucan."

The other men grunted their concurrence to what Benzahr had said.

"She will not be going to Heaven if she is killed today," Lucan said slowly, holding his head with his hands.

"Lucan, are you saying what I think you are saying?" Lex asked in disbelief. His silence said it all.

"What!" exclaimed Eldad. "How could you be that irresponsible? How could you, a guardian, be involved with someone who had not gone through the Wicket Gate?" He shook his head in disbelief.

"It is for situations like this that a rule was made about people we get deeply involved with," Benzahr added. "We can only be closely involved with people who have made that Wicket Gate journey. Now she will be lost to you forever."

Lucan felt an anger rise from deep within him, an anger he hadn't known was there. But rather than cause him to explode, it caused him to calm down. When he spoke, his voice was surprisingly calm and steady. He released his head from his hands and looked at each man, one after the other. "I did not ask to be a guardian. And frankly speaking, with all this now, I am not sure I even want to be one. My life was just fine before this seal came along. And, responsible Mr. Eldad Beriah, need I remind you that this woman was the greatest part of my life before the seal chapter began? With or without your help, gentlemen, I will go and get my woman. Now if you will excuse me, it's getting dark already and I need to be in the Valley of Megiddo by midnight. I have a battle to prepare for."

Without any further word, Lucan left the gathering.

Across town, Gabriel stood inside the living room of a devastated Tara.

"It took my baby, it took my baby," Tara cried out, her tears flowing freely.

"But what did it want?" Gabriel asked. "Did it say anything about her being the child from the experiment of long ago?"

"Have they finally found me after all these years?" Tara lamented. "Why didn't they leave her and take me, Gabriel, why her? You have to help me get her." She held on to his hand as she pleaded with him.

Gabriel put his hand on hers and looked at her tenderly. He felt every ounce of her pain. He said softly, "I need to know if it mentioned anything about her being the child".

"No it didn't," she responded, shaking her head to buttress the point. "But it said something about her boyfriend and a seal and some other seals. Seems it wanted him to bring the seals to it or it would…" She broke down again.

Gabriel allowed her cry for a few moments. Then he probed a bit further. "Did it by chance mention a Guardian of the Seal?"

Tara's head shot up. "How did you know? That's exactly what it said." The sudden look of anxiety that crept onto Gabriel's face caught her attention.
"What is the name of this boyfriend of hers?" he asked.

"Lucan," she answered, "Lucan Belgore."

"Oh No!" Gabriel exclaimed quietly.

For the first time since she had known him, Tara saw him agitated. "What has he done?" she asked. "You know him? What is this whole guardian business? How does it involve Imani? Talk to me Gabriel. And don't tell me I am asking too many questions, because I am not taking that."

Gabriel was already getting up. "I would love to stay and answer your questions, but it's more important we get your daughter back. And if we are going to get her back in one piece, I have to go right away." With that, he squeezed her hand and was gone.

It was a few minutes past ten. Lucan sat in the driver's seat of Imani's flying car, grateful he had it. Even with it, if he would make the Valley of Megiddo on time, he had to leave home immediately. But he had to use it instead of opening a portal to travel. For this battle he had to conserve every ounce of power he had. A few weeks before, if anyone had told him he would be doing anything remotely close to what he was about to do, he would ask the person the title of the book they were reading from. But this was his reality now. He started the engine and let the car hover for a few moments before it rose into the starry night sky.

From the shadows, a dark form rose and followed the car into the sky.

A deep, bare ravine led to the Valley of Megiddo. It had been an olive grove at some point in its history but it was now populated by few trees and a layer of soft, short grass. Lucan glanced at his wrist watch. It was just fifteen minutes before midnight. He landed the car on soft grass and waited in it. At exactly one minute to twelve, he stepped out of the car into the darkness. The air was still and the night warm. All around, sounds of scurrying feet and flapping wings gave evidence to the presence of life there. Suddenly it went eerily quiet. He felt the demons' presence before he actually saw them. The trees seemed to give up whatever spirit trees contained, wilting away. The demons seemed to have appeared out of nowhere, and spread all over the little rock outcrops that surrounded the valley. From their midst, a thin demon with a huge single eye on its massive head stepped forward into the treeless centre of the valley. He had Imani in his grip.

Lucan started forward towards it, but a group of snarling demons blocked his way.

"Let him through," the one-eyed demon, who seemed to be their leader, called out.

The rest of the demons stepped apart to allow Lucan a narrow passage to the centre, where the demon stood with Imani by its side. Lucan reasoned that the demon must have been really convinced that he had resigned to his fate. What nerve!

"Euphrates!" he said out loud and the whole place lit up instantly. All the demons around him were stunned and burst into white flame immediately. The one that held Imani fell backwards, losing his grip on her and she fell on the soft grass. Lucan saw his opportunity and he quickly took it. While they were still incapacitated, Lucan leapt forward, picked Imani up and opened a portal in the same movement. He had to get her away, out of harm's way, before dealing with the demons. The ease with which he had rescued her boosted his confidence that he would easily defeat them. He quickly opened a portal and entered into The Secret Place, placing her on the grass, under a tree. "This is the one place they cannot follow us to. I will be back," he said to her.

"Now to deal with those filthy beasts." He reopened the portal and returned to the Valley.

Still in his changed form, Lucan rose into the sky and did a quick survey of the area. Up in the sky, he shined like one of the stars in the night sky. The demons were many but they were all within the Valley. He sheathed his sword and raised his hands above his head. A barrier of white light formed over the valley, enclosing all the demons within. Then he closed his eyes, summoned all his strength and commanded, "Occupy Euphrates!"

Immediately, the liquid light began to rise within the barrier.

Nimrod had recovered from his initial shock by the time the guardian returned. For a moment, he thought the guardian had escaped him again until the portal opened and the guardian reappeared. It was his lucky day. The girl was not his prize. The guardian was, and he had foolishly returned. Presently, the sea of white light surged towards him and all around, and the agonising cry of demons being consumed filled the air. He spread his leathery wings and began to rise into the sky, towards the guardian. The man's initial bold action had been disconcerting but he would not let a mere human get the better of him the second time. As he approached Lucan, he sent out fiery darts towards him in rapid, crossbow-like bursts. Lucan saw the darts streaking towards him and he dropped his left hand to create a shield of light. The darts bounced harmlessly off the shield. But dropping his hand had caused the barrier to weaken on the left. A barrage of dark, twisty forms escaped the barrier through that weakness, and they quickly writhed away into the darkness. He would seek those out later. Right now, he needed to focus on the new problem that was flying towards him. He raised his hands again and the barrier sealed up. He had seen Gabriel set barriers up, leaving them unattended while he did other things. But he didn't have enough experience to do that. He was already beginning to feel the strain from maintaining the barrier and releasing liquid light simultaneously.

A few other demons followed Nimrod's lead and rose upwards towards the Guardian. They had seen that he couldn't handle the attacks without the weakening of the barrier. From every direction, they sent every manner of missile hurtling towards Lucan. Flaming arrows whistled through the air accompanied by fiery spears with even louder whistles. Clubs, darts, spikes and boomerangs, all flaming, were hurled at him. Lucan had no choice. He was forced to drop both hands and create a barrier around himself to fend the missiles off. The barrier in the valley flickered once and disappeared. The liquid light flowed out into the ravine and screams of demons hiding there - that could not flee its approach quickly enough - rent the air. The missiles hit the barrier around Lucan with fury. He had underestimated their impact. One dart managed to penetrate a weak point on the barrier. A sharp pain rose from his right arm, where it connected to a joint. His armour had taken most of the dart's impact. He wondered how much damage it would have done without the armour. They didn't give him time to dwell on this. The missiles kept coming with unrelenting rapidity. He knew he could not afford to stay holed in. He could hear claws scratching against his barrier now. If he didn't do anything, they would be upon him in no time.

He clasped his hands together and gathered his strength. "Consume, Euphrates," he commanded. The barrier dissolved in a flash and white fire burst out of him, consuming every demon in its path.

Nimrod saw the flash rushing towards him and he erected his own barrier. But the onrushing attack was too strong. In spite of his attempt to repel it, the bolt of light threw him all the way to the ground. He would have been done for if he hadn't erected the barrier. It was clear to him that he had underestimated this guardian. He couldn't win this battle at this level. He looked up into the sky and saw demons falling in every direction as the guardian swung his blazing sword fiercely. Over the years, as Lucifer's top lieutenant, he had grown his powers discreetly, and none of the other lieutenants could really gauge his strength. Now he had no choice but to use his eji form.

Lucan was getting exhausted but he didn't relent one bit. He could not afford to. His sword kept swinging and demons kept disappearing. The initial onslaught from them had reduced into a seemingly more manageable wave of attacks. He was not letting his guard down though. A spear flew past over his head and his hand responded almost reflexively. White light burst from his sword and the demon was gone. Then the waves stopped. For a moment, he thought he had finally got rid of the last of them. But then he could still sense the evil their presence carried within the valley. They were still there. Wondering what they were up to, he decided to stay in the sky rather than float down. Nothing could creep up on him unnoticed up here.

On the ground, all the demons had fled into hiding. Nimrod covered himself in darkness that was darker than even the night, only broken by beads of lava red that crisscrossed the darkness. A thin, big-headed demon entered into the darkness. First to emerge were huge gleaming claws. Then the darkness disappeared to reveal what Nimrod had become. His wiry body had grown in width and short scaly spines covered his whole body. He was longer and larger. The single huge eye had been joined by two more on the sides of the dragon-like head and the single horn had morphed into a crown of horns. He now stood on two pillars for feet and wielded a huge fiery sword. His ribs were bare against stretched leathery skin and pungent smoke was spewing out of his gilled neck. He let out a huge roar and the earth all around shook.

The moment he saw the creature rising out of the ground, Lucan knew this was different from anything he had faced before. As Nimrod rose out of the ground, he swung his sword towards Lucan and a ball of lava tore towards him. Quickly, Lucan moved out of his way. Before Lucan fully stabilised, the demon was beside him and the huge sword was swinging downwards at him. Lucan raised his sword to meet him just in time, blocking the blow. The force with which the demon came down sent Lucas crashing straight to the ground. The shrieks of the excited demons cheering their lord on overwhelmed him. Lucan's adversary landed on the ground and loomed large over him. He needed to buy time to come up with a plan. He raised his sword and white flame shot out of it. But the creature had anticipated this and his huge wings covered it. The flames bounced harmlessly off the wings.

Luckily, Lucan had bought himself time to get on his feet. When the wings unfurled, the demon opened his mouth and out of it flowed a stream of hot lava. Lucan sent out a stream of liquid light out to counter it with a swish of his sword.

But he was already weakening from the hits and lengthy fighting. Soon, the lava began to overpower the light. The stream of lava began to push the river of light back and inch by inch, it gained ground until the light occupied just a small circle inside which Lucan stood. The lava kept pushing, and the beast kept looking at Lucan through eyes that smouldered like live coals.

Lucan summoned all the energy left in him and cried at the top of his voice, "Have dominion, Euphrates!" The river of light burst forth from him again and consumed the lava, expanding to fill the valley once more. The demon could not lift off the ground fast enough. The sea of light caught him and he howled in pain.

But Lucan had reached his limit. After that exertion, he crumpled to the ground, spent. As fast as it had flowed out, the river of light receded back towards him.

Nimrod had been spared. For moments, nothing happened. Nimrod stood in pain at one end and Lucan lay heaving on the ground on the other end. But Nimrod was only momentarily stunned. He recovered and began to walk menacingly towards Lucan, swinging his huge sword. When he got to Lucan, he stood over him and boasted. "You thought you could beat me a second time, you arrogant fool. Your naiveté will cost you everything you wanted to defend. Your woman will be found and when she is, we will usher her unbelieving self into our realm. You will lose your life and seal to us. You will lose everything, human. Now prepare to meet your end."

Nimrod clasped his sword in both hands and raised it above his head. With a mighty roar, he began to swing the sword down. Lucan closed his eyes, resigning to his fate and defeat. He waited for the sword's impact to finish it all. It would hit him any moment now.

But the moment passed and there was no impact. Had the impact been so great that he hadn't felt it before dying and passing on to the next life? He ventured to open his eyes to see what was happening. The sword was less than two feet away from him and he could feel its heat. But it was not moving anymore. A chain of white light was wrapped around the demon's hands, restraining him. His eyes followed the chain of light to its source. Standing atop the highest hill around the valley were the other Guardians of the Seals.

NINE

ex floated down and carried Lucan to the top of the mount where the guardians perched. Eldad restrained the demon with his light chain from where he stood. Once Lucan was safely out of harm's way, the chain disappeared and the demon's fiery sword came crashing down with a colossal force. A huge gash formed where it landed, leaving an ugly scar on the ground.

"That would have been it for the rookie, definitely," Benzahr said to no one in particular through raised eyebrows, hand on chin.

"You came," Lucan said with some effort.

Eldad responded in his usual, boisterous manner, slapping a wincing Lucan heartily on the shoulder. "What kind of comrades would we be if we watched as you threw your life away? Of course we were always going to come."

"And looks like we made it just on time," Lex added.

Benzahr nodded his head in response. The demon was angrily tearing into the sky towards them now and it seemed to have mustered all the others along with it.

"Gentlemen, shall we?" Benzahr asked.

"With pleasure," Eldad responded. "I'll take the horde. You take the leader. Lex, you watch the rookie."

With that, he raised his huge club of light above his head and dived headlong into battle. With Eldad, there were no half measures. Demons soon began flying in every direction, letting out piercing shrieks before dissolving to Tartarus. The demon leader ignored him and kept coming at their mountain top sanctuary. He opened his mouth and sent huge balls of lava speeding towards the guardians. Lex set up a barrier and the balls bounced back into the valley, scorching the demons they landed on. Then Benzahr produced his slim fencer-like sword and stepped into the sky to meet the demon.

The demon let out a disdainful laugh, throwing back his hulking head. He pointed a claw at Benzahr. "You come at me with that needle? You guardians are just pathetic, the lot of you. You mere mortals are unworthy of such power. I will deal with you even quicker than the other fool."

"Hmm" was all Benzahr said with a smile.

"You find this amusing, mortal?" the demon bellowed angrily. "Prepare to meet your end!" With that, he bent his head forward. One of his horns left his head and hovered in the air briefly. Then it began to fly towards Benzahr at a tremendous speed, growing bigger and bigger as it moved through the air. By the time it reached Benzahr, it was as large as a man and exploded like a volcano, covering the whole place with lava and ash.

On the ground, Eldad's hammer kept swinging and demons kept disintegrating and disappearing. He fought like a man possessed until they began to retreat. But unrelenting, he went after them, pummelling them, stunning them and crushing them.

Back in the air, Nimrod was sure he had scored a hit. He didn't bother to wait to see what had happened. There was definitely not going to be anything left of the cocky guardian to see anyway. He prepared himself to go to the hill to finish the other two off. When the ash cleared, the guardian was gone. He had been blown to smithereens. Nimrod let out a burst of laughter. Were these the guardians Lucifer had been so obsessed about?

"And what might you be laughing about?" a voice from behind him asked in a laid back manner.

He spun around. "How? What? When? You…"

"Now, my turn," the guardian said before Nimrod lost sight of him. All Nimrod saw was a blur of light; the guardian's movements were too fast. He felt light touches all over his being and then he found himself falling uncontrollably to the ground. Willing himself to take control of his body, he managed to recover swiftly enough to land on his feet. At first he wondered what had happened to make him fall. He couldn't find any explanation for the great effect of such light touches. Suddenly pain raced through him, causing him to cry out furiously. His wings were gone. He looked around. Where was that damned guardian?

"Looking for me?" the voice came from behind him again.

How did he keep doing that, getting behind him and asking the most annoying questions? It was like the guardian was goading him on with his arrogance-laced voiced.

As for Benzahr, the demon was where he wanted him- on the ground. Benzahr allowed him to turn. The demon swung his huge sword wildly but Benzahr easily evaded it. Skipping forward with the gracefulness of a ballet dancer, Benzahr held his sword vertically upright and said coolly, "Disperse, Gihon." Out of his sword came seven replica swords, all in the seven colours of the rainbow. The swords formed a ring around the demon and the ring followed the demon everywhere he moved. Benzahr watched as the demon tried in vain to get out of the circular spectrum of light, darting here and there, twisting and turning.

"The darkness can never comprehend the light," Benzahr called out to the demon. "Now, be gone, fiend!" Then he drove the sword in his hand into the ground. The other swords burst into a bright aurora of light, lighting up the valley and enveloping the demon where he stood. When the light subsided, the huge demon was gone. Only a sinewy, big-headed form writhed on the floor where the demon had stood.

"So this is your true form," Benzahr remarked. "You must be really strong to withstand my aurora."

Nimrod did not know what had hit him. He only knew he would have been languishing in Tartarus now if he had not set up a last minute barrier. And even then, the force of the guardian's attack had reduced him to his eni form and drained his spirit energy. Now he lay on the floor, completely at his opponent's mercy, unable to fight. He had survived many battles right from the fall and then the creation of this earth, and risen through the ranks in Neatherworld by his own cunning, only to perish at the hand of a mere human. He watched as the guardian took measured steps towards him.

Then out of the darkness behind Nimrod, a burst of red-hot flame shot towards the guardian he had been fighting. The guardian evaded it easily and retreated from Nimrod. Out of the darkness, Beelzebub flew out and the drone of the beating of housefly wings filled the valley.

Nimrod heaved a sigh of relief. He would yet survive. He was about to say something to Beelzebub when more forms began to emerge behind him. First, it was a troll's lumbering form. "Mantov!" Nimrod exclaimed in shock. One by one, all the other demon lieutenants stepped forward. Lilith. Apollyon. Abadon.

Benzahr put some more distance between him and Nimrod to observe what was going on.

The demon lords surrounded Nimrod and Lilith bent over, speaking mockingly. "You look like you've seen a demon, little Nimrod." Her serpentine body shook with laughter as she continued. "Oh, I forgot. We are demons." The others joined her in laughter.

"How did you do it?" Nimrod asked. "You should all be in Tartarus by now. I saw it when you were sent there by that guardian. I saw it with my own eyes." Nimrod was becoming hysterical.

Apollyon snickered. "You really never went beyond being a lowly demon in spite of all the promotions you clawed out from the master. You call yourself a demon lieutenant and yet you believe all you see? Where then is your sense of deceit?"

As they took turns to mock Nimrod, the atmosphere suddenly changed without warning. The already depressing presence of evil brought in by the demon lords became even thicker.

Eldad and Benzahr felt the change too and quickly retreated to the relative safety of the hilltop. A form that Nimrod was familiar with stepped out of the dreadful darkness. All the demon lords bowed in obeisance as the dragon-like form of Lucifer emerged.

"It's a pity to see you like this, Nimrod," Lucifer said through what was intended to be a smile but appeared as a threatening display of razor-sharp teeth. "You undertake to deceive the master of deceit and this simple twist surprises you? I thought you would have some plan to deal with this but you disappoint me! Did you really think my lieutenants were gone and you could now make your move on me? Fool. Imbecilic, basal fool. You were so predictable it was not even interesting to use you as bait and for excitement that would have made it worth my while. You did not even manage to surprise me at any point. You thought I didn't know?"

Raw fear played across Nimrod's eye and he trembled where he lay on the floor. He hoped that his banishment to Tartarus would be done swiftly. But Lucifer continued speaking with a calmness that kept sending a chill down Nimrod's spine. He had seen this before. His punishment would not be swift.

"You were nothing but the bait to draw them out," Lucifer said as he looked towards the mountain and pointed at the guardians. "And what wonderful bait you have been. All four fish were drawn out by you in one swoop. I would have allowed the guardians finish you off, but I need to make an example of you to these other lieutenants." Then he gestured at the demon lords as he continued. "Plus, your friends…" He paused for effect, then continued, "…have requested to give you a 'special' treatment." With that, three demons that had been waiting came forward and carried a shaking Nimrod back to Neatherworld.

Lex watched as horde after horde of demons poured into the valley. This was the single largest amassing of demons he had ever seen anywhere. He looked at the three other men. They seemed to be thinking what he was thinking. What they had faced earlier that night was child's play compared to what they were about to face. It was going to be a very long night. The real battle was just about to begin.

Imani woke up slowly. She had had this interesting dream where a monster had kidnapped her from her mother's house and Lucan had come in shining armour, wielding a big sword, to save her. Then she observed where she was. It was not a dream. Oh God, what had happened to Lucan? She thought they had come there together.

"Finally, you are awake," a male voice said to her.

She turned around and saw a man leaning against the tree she had been sleeping under. He had not been there when she woke up. There was something about him that was vaguely familiar.

"And if you are anything like your mother," he continued, "a barrage of questions is what I'm about to get." He looked at her intently. "So I'll answer the important ones before you ask them. I am Gabriel, an angel and friend to your mother, Tara. Lucan will be safe. And I'm here because you will need my help on the journey you are about to make."

"What journey am I about to make?" she asked, baffled.

"The one you should have made a long time ago, Imani. The one you realise now that you must inevitably make. Now, look deep within yourself. Do you believe?"

Imani understood. "I believe," she said. Nothing happened. Her mother had told her differently. She got on her feet and looked at Gabriel with eyes full of questions. "I thought the path would appear once I confessed my belief?"

Gabriel looked into her eyes again. His gaze seemed to pierce into her soul, gripping her heart.

"Did you really say what your heart was saying?" Gabriel asked. "Close your eyes and listen to your heart. There's a great difference between saying words and confessing them. You must really mean them."

Imani closed her eyes and listened. First she heard the sounds of singing birds. Then she didn't hear them again. Each sound kept going out one by one, as if someone was taking them out, until after a while, all she heard was the flowing of the water of the river on whose banks they stood. It was then that she heard a still, small voice rising from within her. Instinctively, she knew what it was about to say and her mouth moved in sync with it. "I believe that the Wicket Gate is, and it will appear to me now, because I truly desire it from the deepest part of me."

Gabriel whispered softly into her ears. "Open your eyes, Imani."

When she opened her eyes, right in front of her was a huge, gleaming golden gate. "Where did this come from?" she asked, her astonishment animating her face.

She heard Gabriel's voice as if from within her: "The word is near you, even at your lips. Your true belief and confession made the invisible become tangible to you. Now, look harder." Imani peered into the brightness of the gate. She feared it would hurt her eyes, but it didn't. At first, she saw nothing. Then within the huge gate, she saw a smaller gate that was exactly her size and shape - the Wicket Gate, the gate within the gate. Again she heard Gabriel's voice explaining what she was seeing: "The gate is specifically dimensioned for you, ordained from the beginning of time. The big gate is always there, but the Wicket Gate within can only be made manifest by the freewill belief of a human. None else can go through this one, except the one whose belief opened it. Now, go through, Imani."

She felt a little nudge on her back and she began to move towards the gate. With each step she took, the radiance of the gate seemed to infuse her with renewed life. When she eventually touched the gate, she became one with it, and the gate drew her into itself. Then she found herself on a golden stairway. At its top, there were two shinning creatures, each with six wings. One was carrying a golden bowl of white boiling light in its hands and the other had a glowing live coal in its hand. They beckoned on her to climb up to meet them. She quickly scaled the flight of stairs and stood before the creatures. The one bearing the bowl first stepped forward and poured the contents over her wordlessly. She felt herself come truly alive, as if a dormant part of her being had been awakened by the flowing of the light.

Then the other creature flew to her side. It spoke to her as it raised the coal towards her forehead: "This will seal you till we meet again, when you leave earth for the last time. Only those that bear this seal will be allowed into the kingdom." He proceeded to touch her with the coal. As it touched her, she became engulfed in the light again. When the light vanished, she found herself back beside Gabriel on the river bank. He helped her to her feet and said,

"Brace yourself, there's plenty ahead."

"There's more?" she asked.

"Oh," Gabriel responded, "there's so much more."

Gabriel wanted to head straight for the valley of Megiddo, but Imani insisted she must see her mother first. Rather than lose time trying to convince her otherwise, he opened a portal that took them directly to Tara's doorstep. "We have to make this brief," he said to Imani. "You will be unable to explain many things to her at this moment; there just isn't enough time to attempt it."

"Thank you," Imani said as she gave him a big hug.

He smiled. He felt a little of what fatherhood would have been like there and then.

Imani knocked on the door.

"Who's there?" her mother's voice came from within the house. "Imani," she responded.

"Imani?"

They heard the disbelief in Tara's voice. They also heard scrambling as she rushed to the door. When the door flew open, Imani flew into her mother's arms.

Tara kept touching her daughter, as if to assure herself that she was real. "I thought I'd never see you again," she kept saying, "I thought I'd lost you forever." She had thanked Gabriel a thousand and one times and still looked at him intermittently, saying thank you each time. She noticed Gabriel did not sit down.

"I hope you are not in a hurry," she said to him and then turning to Imani, continued, "because there is something I must tell you."

"Actually, we are -" Gabriel was cut off my Imani.

"Actually we are going to hear you out mum."

Gabriel looked from woman to woman. There was a similarity in their expressions. And not for the first time, human freewill stood in his way. He had to wait for them to finish.

"You are not like every other child," Tara began. "You were not conceived the same way that everyone else was." Imani sat up, wondering if her mum would tell her about her father for the first time. She had asked again and again over the years, but it was the one thing Tara refused to talk about.

"You must promise me you will not feel less than a normal human being after you hear this," Tara said.

"Mum, spill it out. I should be able to handle it."

"You never had a father."

Imani squeezed her face in disbelief. "I don't understand. How do you mean? Everyone has a father. If you did not want to tell me, why did you even bring it up?"

Gabriel resigned himself to waiting. This was going to take a while.

The first lights of dawn revealed the utter devastation the colossal battle fought there through the night had brought to the valley of New Megiddo. Everything was scorched. Imani's flying car was nowhere to be found. Tree trunks were charred, split and twisted in a bizarre fashion all over the valley. Deep gullies had formed all over the ground. New, burnt-out caves had been formed on the sides of the surrounding mounts and rocks hewn out of them lay scattered.

All the demon lords were gone, banished into Tartarus forever. Only Lucifer himself remained, and even he had retreated to Neatherworld. The vast hordes of demons that had come in for the battle were all gone, not a single one was left. The toll the battle had exacted on the demons was heavy.

But the guardians had paid a heavy price for the victory. For now, in place of four, Lucan stood alone. The bodies of his fallen comrades lay in a neat row beside him. They had successfully defended their seals from the demons, but they had paid the supreme price. In Lucan's hands, he clutched the prize of the war. He had cried until the tears in his eyes dried out. All of this was his fault. His impetuousness and naiveté had brought this upon them. Each man fell in battle defending him. Lex's word as he fell echoed in his mind "you remind me of Anthony. And of Farida. I finally did right."

They had sacrificed themselves for him. No, he had sacrificed his comrades on the altar of his love for Imani. Imani. The name spurred him to action. He needed to check that she was alright in The Secret Place. He summoned the strength to open a portal and transported himself and his comrades through it to The Secret Place. When they got there, Imani was nowhere to be found. He called out her name in vain, but only the flowing water responded to him. He looked at the lifeless bodies of the once proud Guardians of the Seals. He fell on his knees and cried out again in anguish. They had sacrificed themselves for nothing. "I'm so sorry, I'm so, so sorry," he cried. Where had Gabriel been through all this? Had the angel left them when they needed him most? The grief was too much for him to bear alone. He went through the portal to the mansion where his journey as a guardian had begun, clutching the rest of the seals in his hands and hoping he would find Gabriel there. He needed help immediately; he needed to know that he was not alone. The courtyard where he had first met Benzahr, Eldad and Lex was empty now and the stone palm-shaped seats added to his feeling of aloneness. He had no one in the world now. No angel. No comrades. And most of all, no Imani.

Imani pondered the incredible story her mother had told her as Gabriel bore her through the sky. But it was her story, incredible as it was. She was a child that was totally born of a woman. If anybody could have made it happen, that person was her mother. She couldn't believe her loving mother had once hated men so much that she had devoted her life to making sure women didn't need men again. Her mother had explained her reasoning thus: "The only reason we tolerated men was because we needed their sperm to continue the species. But if someone could remove the need for their sperm, then we could do without them and eliminate all men from the earth. I had made up my mind I would be that someone. What a remarkably-twisted line of reasoning that had been. And to think that I almost made it possible." Tara had said.

Suddenly, a thick mist descended on them out of thin air, and they could see nothing. The moment the mist covered them, Gabriel knew they were not alone. Seconds after the mist came, he heard the droning of wings like a thousand bees coming from the mist. He quickly descended out of the sky, leaving the worst of the mist up in the air. They landed on a small stone bridge over a clear stream. He put Imani safely down and waited for the demon to show himself. It didn't take long for its bee-like form to descend from the mist in the sky. Gabriel could tell immediately that this was no small fry. He set a barrier around Imani quickly. He could afford her no harm. He remembered the devastation on Tara's face when she thought she had lost Imani and the magnitude of the relief on her face when she saw her daughter again. And even though he didn't understand God's master plan fully, he knew that Imani was at the centre of it all. The amount of assaults on her from Lucifer's agents made it abundantly clear that they knew this too.

The demon geared up for his attack. Hundreds of scales dislodged from his wings, hovering above him for a few moments. Then the scales became ignited and flew towards Gabriel like a meteor shower. Gabriel flew into the air to rise above them, but the mist that had brought him down was still in the air. He flew straight into the mist and couldn't see for some moments. When he broke out, the fiery scales were waiting for him. They began blowing up one after the other, creating a chain of explosions. He tried to set up a barrier but he wasn't quick enough. Some of the scales got through the barrier and exploded within it. Gabriel fell to the ground, landing on one knee. He deduced that this had been an attack to size him up. The strength of the explosions had not been very great.

"Hmmm," the demon grunted before opening up his mouth and flicking out a forked tongue twice like a serpent. Without warning, the third time the tongue came out, it kept growing, racing towards the recovering Gabriel the way chameleons used their tongues to get their prey. Gabriel formed a shield of light while still on his knee and fended off the attack. The demon withdrew the tongue. Then he flicked it out again twice and sent it forward the third time. This time, the tongue became red hot and it spun like a drill. Gabriel had gotten to his feet. Again, Gabriel's shield came up to block it. But there was much more force behind this second attack, and it threw Gabriel back, shattering the shield. He checked where Imani was. The barrier around her was still intact. He scrambled to recover his footing, getting set for the next attack. The demon flicked his tongue out twice again. Gabriel braced up. This time when the tongue came flying out, it was covered in a raging inferno, incinerating everything in its path. Gabriel was ready. He drew his sword, and in one lightning swoop, he cut the tongue off. The demon let out a raged howl in pain. The demon was definitely not expecting that.

He spoke to Gabriel for the first time in a grating voice. "For your sword to cut through my attack like that, I have underestimated you grossly. I want to fight you for real now, so I might as well tell you my name. I am Beelzebub, lord of the flying demons. Since I consider you strong enough to know my name, you must tell me yours."

Gabriel shook his head at Beelzebud. He seemed to be as powerful as a demon lord would be, but he was not one of the demon lords Gabriel knew of. "There is no need to tell you who I am," Gabriel said. "What is your purpose?"

The demon laughed derisively. "Since you will be destroyed here, I might as well tell you. The last guardian has all the seals in his possession now and he will soon find the keystone."

"He cannot find the keystone. I am the custodian of the keystone. It is well-hidden," Gabriel said with bravado. But his mind raced to where it laid in the mansion. For the first time in his angelic existence, he questioned if he had heard God's instruction correctly.

"That is what you think, but you underestimate my lord Lucifer, the greatest schemer who sees multiple steps ahead of all his foes. You will be surprised, angel without a name. And when Lucan finds it, what do you think he will do?"

"He will not find it!" Gabriel said emphatically.

"You angels have not studied humans as well as we have, you do not know them as well as we do. Lucan feels he is alone, with no one in this world. We have driven him to the point of despair. He blames his carelessness for the loss of his comrades and the inadequacy of his strength for the loss of his woman. A heart in despair will cling to anything that will soothe its despair. There is only one direction we want him to turn in his despair, and we must keep him in that state for long enough for him to make that choice, since he has his blasted freewill. The woman you take to him will break the hold of this despair over him. We cannot have that happen, so I must stop you, and the woman. It is that simple." With that, Beelzebud spread his wings and began to beat them vigorously. As he did, he began to transform. Gabriel wondered what the demon's eji form would look like. He did not have to wonder for too long. When the transformation was complete, a huge wasp-like creature, much larger than the initial housefly form, hovered before him. The tail was elongated and curved forward like that of a scorpion. It waved the tail from side to side twice.

The third time, it sent the tail flying towards Gabriel at supersonic speed. Gabriel's shield came up just in time to meet it. Then, without warning, out of the mist from above, an exact replica of the tail came flying downwards. Gabriel stumbled backwards, managing to dodge the second tail. Where had that come from? He was sure it had only one tail and that was the one he blocked. He didn't have the time to ponder. Again, the tail whipped twice, and then it flew towards him, this time even faster and covered in flames. Gabriel raised his sword again and cut through the tail. But from the mist, again came another replica burning tail. This time, he couldn't sidestep it. His barrier came up a second too late; the attack was just too fast. It hit him on the right side, tearing through his armour and charring the shining armour black on that side. He fell on one knee for the second time in this battle. He could not afford to take another hit. He needed the girl's help, so he said to her being, "Pray."

Imani heard Gabriel's earnest request within her heart. But pray for what? She had been watching the battle from where she stood, within the barrier. The demon clearly had Gabriel on the back foot; it was winning. Gabriel had not even been able to attack it just once. He had only been defending.

Gabriel seemed to sense her confusion. "Listen to your heart," he said to her. "You will know what to say."

She reached deep within. The noise of the ongoing battle kept distracting her. She struggled to shut it out but she couldn't. "You have the seal from the Wicket Gate now, pray." That was all she heard, and it was Gabriel speaking earnestly again as he dodged another attack from the demon. She closed her eyes. She didn't need to shut the noise out. She reached deep within herself again and then, as if they had always been there, the words came to her. It was as though her heart was speaking them as her lips moved. "Let the limits be removed. Let the fullness be released now of my guardian angel."

Beelzebub prepared for his final attack on the angel. He had overestimated the angel; his eji release was definitely not needed to defeat this one. He waved his tail twice to gather energy into it. He channelled the energy and the flame on it grew into raging proportions like none he had ever created before. He wanted this to finish the angel off. On the third wave, he shot the tail forward. The angel was not attempting any defence. He had resigned to his fate, Beelzebub figured. He would make the angel's demise quick then. He increased the flames even further, giving it everything he had to incinerate his opponent at one go.

Even though the flaming tail was flying speedily towards him, Gabriel heard Imani's prayer. As an archangel, he had to place a limit on his powers while on earth on assignment. Only the freewill prayer of a human being or express orders from God Himself could permit him to remove the limit. He clasped his hands together and exclaimed, "Release!"

Immediately, he was wrapped in the true light of Heaven. He grew to nearly four times the human size he had been, his armour gleaming like a collection of suns. He had in his hand a sword of white light and crackling lightning ran along its shaft. His six wings were flaming white as was his hair. The demon's tail hit him but he felt nothing. He spoke to the demon: "You wanted to know my name somewhat desperately. I am Gabriel, who stands before the very throne of God, archangel of the cherubim and guardian angel of Israel. Now, this is the end, Beelzebub, lord of the flies!"

The demon let out a frightened shriek and tried to retreat into the mist.

"No, you are not getting away," Gabriel bellowed. With that, he swung his sword upwards in the demon's direction. A beam of white light went out of the sword and hit the demon. Instantly, the demon was gone, disintegrated by the light.

Gabriel hoped they were not too late to reach Lucan.

Lucan stood in the middle of the courtyard. He had been thinking. If only he could see his comrades one more time, he would be able to say how sorry he really was. As he kept thinking about this, another thought entered his consciousness. There was something about it he couldn't quite wrap his mind around, but it was a true thought and so he waved the uneasiness aside. His fallen comrades were guardians and would have gone straight to heaven after their death. Were they not the ones that said death was not the end? He could still see them again. He had all the seals. He closed his eyes and began the chant:

"Out of the east

Out of Eden

Four flow as one

One parts into four

Baruch, Baruch

Arise and flow.

Euphrates!"

Then he felt the familiar rush of his seal's fusion with him, transforming him into his guardian state. But he was not done yet. He had all the seals and would do something that had not been done since Jacob. He clasped his hands together and continued. "Gihon!" he shouted. An unfamiliar energy flowed into him. Yet he continued. "Pishon! Tigris!" He said those in quick succession. For the first time in millennia, the four seals were fused with one person. The power he had felt when he had only the Euphrates seal was nothing compared to what he felt now. There was only one piece of the puzzle he didn't have yet. But Lucan willed himself to unite with the keystone, just as it had been at the beginning when Jacob possessed both the seals and the keystone. Closing his eyes still, he visualised the keystone. "Take me to it," he said softly.

When he opened his eyes, he found himself in an almond grove beside a small river. There was an ancient stone altar there, and he recognised this as Jacob's altar. He did not know which of the stones of the altar was the keystone. They all looked exactly the same. "The guardian has come, reveal yourself!" he commanded. There was a rumbling in the altar and suddenly, it crumbled in one explosion. It was so sudden that Lucan could not get out of the way in time. Where the altar had been, a stone sat. Gingerly, he reached out to touch the stone, expecting it to explode like the altar did. There was indeed an explosion, but it was not the stone that exploded. The burst of life force that entered into Lucan as his fingers touched the stone nearly threw him off balance. A column of light then rose from the stone into the sky. A stairway spiralled away upwards and heaven opened up above him just as it had done with Jacob, the first guardian on that fateful night.

Without warning, a blast hit the area where Lucan stood and the almonds were incinerated in an instant. The power of the seals protected him from the impact but he felt their presence immediately. All around, there was a vast, innumerable company of demons. At the head of the throng was Lucifer himself, in his eni form.

"Where did you come from?" Lucan queried Lucifer.

Lucifer laughed derisively. "You have been of more service to me than the best of my demons, Mister Lucan Belgore."

Lucan responded angrily. "That's a lie! All you do is spew out dirty lies, and this one is your biggest lie yet, you king of lies."

Lucifer laughed again. "You can call me whatever you want and say absolutely anything you like. But you have just led me to the object of thousands of years of unfruitful searching and scheming. Did you think you really survived that battle in the valley of Megiddo because we couldn't kill you? There was just you, and there were still many of us. If we really wanted to kill you, you would have been dead long ago. But we let you survive. And in your usual way, you didn't pause to think why. You should have figured out that this was so because we knew you could lead us here. And that is exactly what you have done. No matter how powerful you have become Lucan, you stand alone against this host. You stand no chance whatsoever. It would be best for you to step aside and let us pass in and maybe I could consider sparing you."

Lucan quickly set up a strong barrier around the entrance of the portal. He had yet again been a fool. These demons had outsmarted him at every turn, every single time. "You will only get in over my dead body," he responded defiantly.

Lucifer flashed his blood-thirsty teeth. "I was hoping you would say that, Lucan."

Lucan raised one arm and swung it in the direction of the demons. A wave of light went out of the sword, and a huge swath of demons disappeared.

"Impressive, truly impressive," Lucifer remarked. "But how long can you sustain the use of a power you are so new to using? It will soon drain your strength and then what?"

As Lucifer spoke, Lucan felt his strength truly ebbing away. He had not rested since the previous night when he had initially set out to save Imani. He had taken more than a hit in that battle and his body was already strained. The new powers were placing an even greater strain on him now. But he decided he would keep pushing on. He remembered Lex's words: "With great power comes great responsibility." He had to win this battle somehow, against the odds.

Gabriel reached Benzahr's mansion and put Imani down. The flight had dizzied her a bit so he set her on one of the hand-shaped stone seats. Lucan was not there. But Gabriel was certain he had been there. This was the point where he had felt the power of the seals unleashed just before Beelzebub appeared to delay him. That was why he had come there straight after the battle. Had he come too late? This was what he was thinking when he felt the release of a very familiar power. It was unmistakable. The portal had been opened. He felt its energy right away; there was not even the faintest of barriers around it. And a huge concentration of demons had gathered there. "Lucan!" he exclaimed. He opened a portal and headed for the almond cove. He was halfway through before realising he had left Imani behind. He quickly backtracked and called out to her to follow him.

The fatigue was beginning to take its toll on Lucan. The stress of maintaining the barrier around the portal and fighting the demons at the same time was enormous. Waves of attacks kept coming at him relentlessly. The fear of their master's wrath if they hesitated superseded the fear of the destruction Lucan meted out to them. In his already weakened state, the magnitude of it all drained him faster than he had imagined it would. Yet, Lucifer himself had not attacked him. He was deliberately sending the lesser demons into the battle to wear him out until he was ready to take Lucan down himself.

Suddenly, the barrier around the portal flickered. It was the signal that Lucifer had been waiting for. He sensed that Lucan was sufficiently weakened for his final assault. Stirring himself, he began to move towards Lucan. The ground shook with each step he took. Demons cowered and quickly scurried out of his path. The smoke that oozed from his chest pipes darkened the sun.

He produced a huge, dark chain that he had specially prepared for this time. Moving faster than Lucan could react in his weakened state, Lucifer thrust the chains over his shoulders on both sides. The chain drove itself deep into the ground at both ends, anchoring Lucan to the spot.

As soon as the chain touched him, Lucan knew he was in big trouble.

Then Lucifer taunted him. "Don't struggle, Lucan, you only make the draining faster when you do. Or maybe you should struggle."

Lucan kept trying to shrug it off, but he had used up too much strength in the battles. He struggled in futility until the chain finally drained him of his last powers. As the last ounce of strength left him, the barrier around the entrance to the portal shattered.

"This chain can only be broken by one as strong as I am," Lucifer said as he stood before Lucan. "But in this state, you are not. There are only a few others in the entire universe who can. I'm afraid none of them is here with you. And they will soon be too preoccupied with a fight more important than your insignificant self. So you are totally hopeless, Lucan. No one will help you. No one will come for you. You will watch now as I make my triumphant entry into heaven to reclaim my place, all thanks to your good service."

"You will fail," Lucan breathed weakly.

"Oh, we will see about that," Lucifer growled. Then he turned to the demons and proclaimed in a thunderous voice: "Now, we go to take what is rightfully ours. Come, let's go up. The Tree of Almightiness awaits you. You will be as gods!" The demons responded with an equally deafening shout.

As Lucan watched in despair, Lucifer led his horde up the stairs through the portal. Lucan closed his eyes and bowed his head in deep sorrow. Again, he had caused the unthinkable. Again, he was all alone.

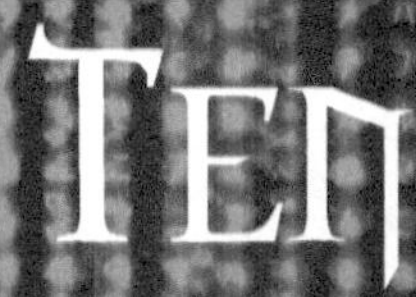

ucifer burst out at the other end of the portal with his snarling horde behind him. He looked around. The scenery of the place was familiar. "Eden of the East," he remarked, "so this is where you have been hidden all along."

Knowing the resourcefulness of the race of men, Lucifer had always wondered why they never discovered Eden of the East in all their quests for the Tree of Life on earth. They had called it all sorts of names – the Elixir of Life, the Holy Grail, the Fountain of Youth and many others. But they had never found it. Now he knew why. He became overwhelmed with nostalgia. The place brought back memories.

A voice he was familiar with but had not heard in ages called out to him. "Welcome, Lucifer."

He lifted his eyes and saw an archangel standing alone a short way off. His six wings and blazing armour signified that he was the top of the seraph order that Lucifer himself had once belonged to.

"We meet again, Michael, Captain of the Heavenly Hosts," Lucifer said with a hint of teasing. "It's indeed been a while. I expected a larger welcome party. Have all your hosts deserted you already at the sound of my approach that you come out here all alone? And they said I was the arrogant one."

"Alone?" Michael responded, waving his hands. "Has your ambition blinded you that much?" Then, as if out of nowhere, the Heavenly host materialized behind him. Chariots of fire. Six-winged seraphs bearing flaming swords. Cherubim archers bearing golden bows and arrows. Two-winged angels with all manners of weapons. And in a single file in the front row, all the generations of the Guardians of the Seals; from Jacob, all the way down to Eldad, Benzahr and Lex, took position. They bore weapons that had been theirs during their earthly existence. A bright splendour emanated from the whole host, directly contrasting the seething, thick darkness oozing out from the invading mass of demons that stood before them.

Lucifer turned and addressed his demons. "This is the time we have been waiting for. Brace yourselves and forget all the former defeats. We will overcome and rule this place. Unlimited power awaits those that fight valiantly. Eternal torment awaits the cowardly. We will not retreat. We will not be defeated. Remember, one of you here will partake of the Tree of Almightiness with me. Fight to be that one!"

The demons let out a great shout.

"Let's give them hell!" Lucifer thundered.

Shouts of "give them hell, give them hell" erupted from the demons. Riding on the momentum of their cries, they charged forward.

Lucan stood helpless before the open portal, pinned to the spot by Lucifer's chains. His mind was filled with all sorts of imaginations of the battle he was sure he had ignited now that Lucifer had gone up into Heaven. Suddenly, he heard Imani's voice calling his name. He waved it aside. His mind must be playing tricks on him, especially now that he was on the precipice of unconsciousness. Delirium was setting in. Then he saw a flash of light, and his chains fell off. He collapsed to the ground, drained of all his strength, immobile. Someone rushed to his side and helped him off the floor, calling his name over and over again. When he opened his eyes, he saw the face he had longed for in the last couple of hours, the face he had thought was lost to him forever. "Imani," he said, touching her on the cheek. "It's really you. Am I dreaming? Or maybe I have died and I'm now in Heaven?"

"I'm here Lucan, I'm really here, in flesh and blood," Imani responded.

"I thought I had lost you." Lucan said.

Tears of joy streamed down Imani's face as she cradled him. He saw that Gabriel too was there. Lucan was grateful he was not alone after all. Lucifer had lied. But this was not the Gabriel he was used to seeing. This Gabriel radiated a different level of power and he had grown very huge. "Thank you," Lucan said to the angel, "thank you so much."

"There is much that you must tell me, Lucan," Gabriel said. "And there is much you must know. Lucifer?"

Lucan lowered his weary eyes. "He got in… along with a vast army of demons. Is…is all lost now?"

Gabriel would have none of that kind of talk. "Break out of this despair, Lucan," he said. "That chain that held you bound fed on your despair. It was the despair that drained your power, not the chain itself. All cannot be lost. All these things will work together for good."

Lucan raised his head. "Really? This can still be turned around?"

Imani reached for his hand and squeezed it. Lucan turned from Gabriel and looked into her eyes.

"Yes Lucan," Imani assured. "Yes, we can still turn this around. Only if we believe. Close your eyes and listen to your heart alone. What does it say?"

Lucan closed his eyes. Immediately, he began to hear familiar voices telling him just how hopeless the situation was and how he was to blame for it. With a supreme effort of his will, he pushed the voices aside and silenced them. And then he listened. At first, he heard nothing; it was all quiet within. Then, out of the quiet, he heard a voice he had never heard before, a still small voice. Then his lips moved in sync with the voice within, saying, "I believe."

Gabriel smiled. There was yet hope. "Stand aside for a moment," he said to Imani. "This Guardian of the Seals will yet fight." Then he turned to Lucan. "Stand to your feet, Lucan Belgore."

Imani helped Lucan up on his feet and then went to stand behind Gabriel. Gabriel stepped forward before Lucan, towering greatly above him. From Gabriel's belt, he produced a vial containing waters from the river of The Secret Place. "These waters will heal your wounds and revive your body," he proclaimed as he poured the content of the vial over Lucan. Lucan felt life restored to him again as the water flowed down his body. Then Gabriel continued, "Now, become the true Guardian of the Seals once again."

Together, angel and man chanted the words that would release the seal.

Out of the east

Out of Eden

Four flow as one

One parts into four

Baruch, Baruch

Arise and flow

Euphrates. Tigris. Gihon. Pishon.

One more time that day, the power of the four seals became unified in Lucan. His armour shone as brightly as Gabriel's and his sword was as pure light. Re-energised, he turned towards the portal. Then he looked back and beckoned on both Gabriel and Imani. "Let's go."

Up in Heaven, the battle raged on fiercely. The angels outnumbered the demons five to one, but the demons were fighting ferociously, spurred on by a mixture of fear of their master and an intense hatred of the angels. Seeing the angels reminded the demons of their former status, that glorious status they had before they followed Lucifer in rebellion in the early days. Most of the lush vegetation in Eden of the East was being razed to the ground, leaving only charred remains on the landscape. Bright flashes blazed everywhere as the fiery weapons wielded by both sides clashed. Swords slashed, arrows whistled, clubs crushed, scythes were swung, spears were thrust and flames shot out of bare hands. The demons kept coming like a crazed horde but the angels held their lines. Wave after wave, demons came screaming ferociously, but the angels kept repelling them. With every clash between the two forces, the demons took heavy losses. Some angels and demons had taken the battle into the air and the fighting was as heavy there as it was on the ground. Flaming bodies kept falling to the ground from above. The vast majority of the fallen bodies belonged to the demons. The tide would rise and then abate whenever the demons suffered defeat. Still, Lucifer would rally them with his promise of eternal glory and they would regroup and rush forward again. But as the fighting went on, Lucifer could tell that his forces were being depleted fast. He admitted to himself that he had come to the battle with weak demons. The very thing that had held his kingdom together in their time in Neatherworld was now his undoing. In maintaining the atmosphere of fear that had been essential to his rule, he had banished the most powerful demons he had to Tartarus. Now, it fully dawned on him that he was the only truly powerful demon remaining. His weak demons were no match for the angels they fought. Every time the demons surged forward, it was only a suicidal attempt at fighting.

Michael suddenly gave a shout and the angels began an offensive against the demons and counter-attack. A hail of flaming arrows from the cherubs whistled through the air. All around Lucifer, demons burst into flames. Before Lucifer's diminishing horde could recover from this sudden assault, the chariots of fire charged forward. The demons scattered into disarray in the face of the angelic onslaught. The fear of the approaching angels overrode their fear of Lucifer and they began to flee to the mouth of the portal to escape back to earth.

"Useless vermin," Lucifer barked. He rose into the air and poured out a stream of pure darkness from his chest pipes towards the angels. The frontline of angels could not stop on time, so they entered the darkness. It swallowed them up totally, and they were not seen again. The advancing angels halted, wary of the almost living darkness before them. Behind Lucifer, the first set of demons had reached the mouth of the portal. As they prepared to dive in, a huge flaming sword came out from the portal, cutting them down. Out of the portal, Gabriel emerged first, followed by Lucan and Imani.

On the other front of battle, Michael rose into the air from the ranks of angels and addressed Lucifer. "You forget that I am here. Your tricks will not work." Then Michael raised his sword and shot a great bolt of light into the darkness. The light and darkness, like two great dragons warring, collided, and the light swallowed up the darkness. The guardians, who had been watching all along, then joined in the battle and beat the darkness back until it was no more. With that, Michael issued a command for another charge and the angels, now joined by the guardians, advanced once more. Then Michael faced up to Lucifer and shot a blast from his sword at him. "This is the end, son of the morning."

Lucifer raised his great wings and absorbed Michael's blast. He surveyed what was going on below with a quick glance. What remained of his forces was being cut down at the front by the angels and at the rear by Gabriel and Lucan. Soon, he would be alone to face all three forces. He wouldn't stand a chance against all three at once. But he was Lucifer and he would find a way out. A thought crept into his mind. "The Word can never be broken," he said to Michael. "My end cannot come now. My end is not in your hands."

"Your forces are totally defeated," Michael responded. "You stand alone now. This, indeed, is your end."

"But you forget something," Lucifer retorted. "You forget the pronouncement of my end in the garden. It will not be at the hand of any angel, not even at the hand of God himself. His beloved humans are the only ones who have that power. Even then, only one of them can - the Seed of the Woman. I do not see this seed around. So, will you disobey and in ending me, become just like me?"

With that, their swords clashed, sending sparks flying all over.

"You know less than you think you know, Lucifer," Michael said.

Lucifer fell back from Michael. What was he talking about? "Why are you speaking but yet saying nothing to me?" Lucifer replied angrily. "You dare not attempt to break the Word or you become mine. No matter how many times you say it, this is not my end!"

Gabriel had risen into the air to Michael's side while Lucifer was speaking.

"It's been a while, Lucifer," Gabriel said amiably.

On the ground, Lucan was finishing the last of the demons off. Lucifer maintained his distance from the two archangels. Why did they not attack him? What were they planning? It must be the Word that was restraining them.

Gabriel seemed to latch on to his thoughts. "Are you wondering why we are not fighting you?"

Lucifer did not bother to humour him with a response.

But Gabriel continued: "Our purpose here is done. The rest of the battle belongs to men and it is they that must get the victory." Then he pointed down at Lucan.

"How do I know this is not some gimmick to attack me while I'm distracted?" Lucifer asked skeptically, confusion setting in. "I have fought this one before and he wasn't much to fight."

Like a flash, Michael appeared beside Lucifer, startling him. "You forget who we are, Lucifer. Lies belong to you and your kind. Be rest assured that you will find this fight to be a very different one."

Lucan watched as Lucifer slowly descended out of the sky and stood opposite him. The voices of fear within him began to rise again, but he shut them out quickly.

"We meet one more time, Lucan Belgore," Lucifer roared. "And something tells me it will be our last meeting."

Lucan nodded in agreement. "On that we agree. It will surely be our last."

The host of angels and the line of generations of guardians stood by to watch the battle that was about to unfold before them. Imani held on to Gabriel. Every being seemed to hold its breath. This was the decisive moment, when the fate of men would be decided.

Lucan raised the first weapon in his arsenal. A club of light. Eldad's.

Lucifer clapped his hands and black flames raced towards Lucan. Lucan stretched his free hand and white light burst out of his hands to meet the black flames. For a moment, the light seemed to have stopped the flames. But the flames began to absorb the light and grow bigger. Lucan closed his eyes and listened. The voice said one word. Fear. He had to meet this adversary headlong like Eldad would. He raised his club and charged into the black flames with a shout. Waving the club before him, he beat a path to Lucifer through the flames. Lucifer swung his fiery sword at him, but Lucan sidestepped it and brought the club crashing down on Lucifer's side. The impact stunned Lucifer and sent him reeling backwards. Lucan rushed forward to land another hit. But as Lucifer careened, he sent a hail of fiery darts to meet Lucan. Lucan tried to fend them off with his shield, but they evaded his shield and went right around him, exploding on him from behind. The pain tore through him and made him fall face down to the ground. As he tried to recover, he got up slowly, slightly dazed. When he looked around, there were seven Lucifers surrounding him.

"If you could not handle only one…" one of them taunted.

"How will you fight seven?" another one continued.

"You are doomed!" a third one shouted at him.

They all began to close in on Lucan, their fiery swords raised. "You are doomed!" they chanted loudly.

Lucan sought to block the voices out but he seemed to hear them from within and they drowned out everything else in his heart and mind. As the Lucifers closed in on him, the evil they oozed began to choke him. He raised a barrier around him to stop them, but they passed right through it as if it was not there. He tried to move to attack, but he was rooted to the spot. "What is this?" he asked, angry but perplexed. "What have you done to me?"

Gabriel had to resist the urge to jump into the battle to help Lucan. He had given his word and had orders from above not to interfere in this. He turned to Imani. Concern was written clearly all over her face. "You will help him, but you must wait," he said to her. "Are you ready?"

"Yes Gabriel, I will," Imani replied. "I just fear that if I keep waiting, the time may never come."

"You must believe in him, Imani."

Imani sighed. "Okay, I will not doubt."

Out of nowhere, Lucan heard the words. He repeated them to himself, "I will not doubt." It felt as though his feet were being unhinged from the ground as he spoke the words. He bolted out of the circle of the seven Lucifers roaring those words, catching them by surprise.

"This is for Benzahr," he cried out aloud, eyes closed. With that, the club he was carrying disappeared. In its place, a fencing sword of light materialised in his hands. The Lucifers had recovered from the surprise and come around him again, this time moving faster to trap him in their circle. But in this stance and with this weapon, Lucan was faster, and he escaped upwards.

"Disperse Gihon," he commanded. One after the other, seven swords rapidly came out of his sword. The swords formed a ring around the Lucifers, one behind each. Each of them tried to strike the swords but their fiery swords just passed through the swords of light harmlessly.

"The darkness,' Lucan said fiercely, thrusting the white sword into the ground from above, "cannot comprehend the light!"

The huge aurora resulting engulfed all seven Lucifers in one blinding instant. When the blaze died down, only one Lucifer was standing.

Enraged, Lucifer flew at Lucan. "I will crush you, mortal and not a single piece of you will be found!"

Lucan quickly discarded the slender Gihon sword for his own big Euphrates sword. Lucifer's sword clashed with it, and the impact sent Lucan flying into a tree. Before he could recover, Lucifer's tail had come swinging downwards. Lucan quickly put up a barrier. He would have been crushed if the tree hadn't taken the brunt of the tail's force as the tail broke through the tree and barrier. Lucan tried to rise into the air for some reprieve but as he left the ground, a double-fisted attack from Lucifer beat him back to the ground. It was as if Lucifer was everywhere at the same time.

Lucifer stood over Lucan. "To send a mere mortal against me! Die, Lucan!" He raised his sword to finish him off.

But from where he lay, Lucan breathed, "encircle Pishon." Out of the ground, before Lucifer, a chain of light burst forth and wrapped around Lucifer's sword, restraining it from coming down. Another wrapped around his legs. Then another around his arms. Lucifer could not move; he became rooted to the spot. Lucan got up slowly and addressed Lucifer. "This chain is called faith. Until my last breath, I know and believe that I will yet have victory over you, no matter how bad it seems." Then he moved in a flash and cut Lucifer's wings off.

Lucifer howled in pain and rage. Every time he seemed to have the guardian cornered, the blasted human came up with something. The rage caused him to ignite and he transformed into a being of pure fire. He had been called out of fire, and fire was his true nature. The heat was so great that the beings that had been watching moved back, further away from the battle. Only Michael and Gabriel stayed put.

Lucifer turned to them and addressed all of them: "I am Lucifer, son of the morning, brightest of the stars. Called out of fire, behold my glory and tremble at my fury. Not many have seen it, but all who did became mine. You will all bow to me. For I am the greatest of the angels, the greatest of any being ever made."

Lucan shot a bolt of light at him. It hit him in the back but bounced off harmlessly. "You might be the greatest creature," Lucan responded to Lucifer, "but you were made and can never be equal to the Maker." Lucan gripped his sword with both hands and pointed it at Lucifer. "I am your opponent. Do not turn your back until the battle is over." The words had barely come out of his mouth fully when a river of fire raced towards him from Lucifer. Everything in its path turned to ashes the moment the river of fire touched it. "Flow, Euphrates!" Lucan commanded. A river of light flowed out of him to meet the river of fire. But the fire consumed the light rapidly and kept racing towards Lucan. Lucan raised the club and went out to meet the fire. But the moment the club touched it, it turned to ashes. Lucan quickly rose into the air to escape the fire. Nothing seemed to be able to stop the all-consuming fire.

As Lucan rose into the air, a force he could not see began to push him down until he landed back on the ground. He tried to get back up but this powerful unseen force kept him pinned to the ground. The river of fire flowed ever so close. He was convinced that the moment it touched him, he would go up in flames.

Imani could not bear to watch any longer. Lucan was truly about to die and none of the angels, not even Gabriel was intervening. They said they could not interfere. Well, she was not an angel, and neither had she promised anything of that nature. So, determined, she broke out from Gabriel's side and raced to where Lucan was. Just as the flames were about to cover Lucan, she threw herself over him to shield him with her body. Although she was acting on instinct and knew it would not save Lucan, she did it anyway. The flames submerged them both, and then it continued to flow forward for some time.

Lucifer turned to Gabriel and Michael, mocking them. "How touching. The guardian's lover chose to die with him. I told you before, my end is yet to-"

A blast from behind knocked him forward.

"How many times do I have to tell you not to turn your back on me?" Lucan's voice came from behind him.

Lucifer turned around slowly in disbelief. "How did you…you could not…"

Imani helped Lucan sit up. Then she left him and began to walk towards Lucifer in measured strides. Gabriel moved to stop her but Michael held him back. "It is all in the plan," he said.

"What is this?" Lucifer asked aloud in irritation, looking at Gabriel and pointing at Imani. "Is this all you have left?"

Imani kept on coming towards him until she stood right before him. Compared to her the great leviathan was like a mountain.

"I am Imani," she said to Lucifer. "I am born of a woman, born without a father. Today you meet your doom, Lucifer, for I am the Seed of the Woman." A murmur went through all the host watching.

"You are a mere woman!" Lucifer retorted. "By the guardian's strength, you somehow survived and you are now trying to buy time for him."

Imani did not respond. The thoughts flowed through her as if she had been present through every event that had happened throughout time. She did not need to learn anything. She immediately knew things. She clasped her hands and began to chant.

> Out of the east
>
> Out of Eden
>
> Four flow as one
>
> One parts into four
>
> Baruch, Baruch
>
> Arise and flow.

Lucifer watched in disbelief as she transformed before his eyes into a shining one. The power that radiated from her surpassed even that of the archangels behind him.

"What are you?" Lucifer asked, his voice quaky with fear. "You cannot be what you claim to be. This must be some form of trick!"

"We did not survive your attack," Imani responded. "But you forgot that we were mortal beings. We died. For Lucan, a guardian, death is a transformation from mortality to immortality. Death, for a guardian, is not the end. He is here among the rank of fallen guardians."

Lucifer looked and saw that Lucan had joined the rest of the guardians, who were standing amongst Heaven's hosts. Lucifer looked back at Imani angrily as she continued speaking. "The greatest expression of love is sacrifice," she said. "I made the supreme sacrifice with my life out of my love for Lucan. As I held him and we died, the seals spoke to me. Their true purpose is to empower the Seed of the Woman, and that is me. The guardians have been the seals' custodians, and they have held them for years, waiting for me. When my life was given out of love, I truly became the Seed of the Woman. Except a seed of corn dies, it abides alone. Once it dies, it produces a large crop. You have heard it said in this place but I will say it again. This truly is the end for you, Lucifer, son of the morning."

"No, never!" Lucifer shouted. "I will prevail. I have killed you once. Now, die again!" He unleashed the river of fire again, directly over her. But it was of no effect. She was unscathed. Lucifer tried again and again, but she walked out of each as if he had done nothing.

"Why do you do the same thing over and over again?" she asked, waving her hands. Massive chains of light appeared out of nowhere around Lucifer. They began to bind him from head to toe. He struggled and twisted to break free from them with all of his might. But the more he struggled, the tighter the chains became.

"These chains are called love," Imani proclaimed. "It is the most powerful force whether in Heaven or on the earth. Your struggles are useless against it." As she spoke, Lucifer's flames were snuffed out and he was reduced to his eni form. He fell like a log to the ground. Then Imani raised her hand and a sword of pure white light appeared in it out of thin air.

"Multiply," she commanded. Immediately, seven identical swords of white light surrounded Lucifer where he lay. "The darkness can never comprehend the light," she said coolly. The pure white light swallowed Lucifer up totally.

When it cleared, Lucifer was no more.

A great shout of victory erupted from the Heavenly host. They rushed and lifted Imani off her feet, cheering as they brought her to the archangels.

When they had set her down, Imani turned to Gabriel. "What happens now that Lucifer is destroyed?" she asked. "Will evil disappear from creation finally?"

Gabriel fell on a knee to be closer to her. "We must believe in men," he said. "The world is free of Lucifer, but the seed of evil in the hearts of men will persist. We must believe that without Lucifer's nurture, men will finally overcome the evil within."

"And the portal?"

"The seals have fulfilled their purpose. The portal will now be closed forever. Men will be able to come into Heaven only by the Wicket Gate. But the portal does have one final use before it is sealed up forever."

"What use?"

"Turn around," Gabriel answered.

Imani did a quick one-eighty. Two angels were just setting her mother down at the edge of the portal. Imani ran to her and they locked in warm embrace wordlessly for moments, tears flowing freely. "Well done my daughter," her mother whispered into her ears. "In a little while, we'll be together again." Then she kissed Imani's forehead and let go.

Tara turned to Gabriel and said, "Thank you. For everything."

A few moments later, the angels that had brought Tara helped her out through the portal. Imani watched the mouth of the portal until the angels that went with Tara returned. Then Gabriel went to the portal and sealed it forever.

When Imani turned around, it was to face a smiling Lucan. He stretched forth his hands.

"Let's go home," he said.

Smiling also, she held his hands and together they took their place amongst the Heavenly hosts.